"You need me,"

Shawna insisted.

"You're the only one who thinks so." Gabriel put a hand to her cheek, satin-smooth, and traced a finger along the line of her jaw.

"What?" she whispered.

"Just give me another minute." Self-recrimination already sang in him, but he pulled her into his arms. He was somehow convinced that the taste of her, too, would be unique—sunshine, heat and promise. And he had to know.

He wanted to feel again. He wanted to touch again. But it was more than that. It had to be *her*.

And that changed everything.

Dear Reader,

Happy holidays! In honor of the season, we've got six very special gifts for you. Who can resist *The Outlaw Bride,* the newest from Maggie Shayne's bestselling miniseries THE TEXAS BRAND? Forget everything you think you know about time and how we move through it, because you're about to get a look at the power of the human heart to alter even the hardest realities. And you'll get an interesting look at the origins of the Texas Brands, too.

ROYALLY WED, our exciting cross-line continuity miniseries, continues with Suzanne Brockmann's *Undercover Princess.* In her search to find her long-lost brother, the crown prince, Princess Katherine Wyndham has to try life as a commoner. Funny thing is, she quite likes being a nanny to two adorable kids—not to mention the time she spends in their handsome father's arms. In her FAMILIES ARE FOREVER title, *Code Name: Santa,* Kayla Daniels finds the perfect way to bring a secret agent in from the cold—just in time for the holidays. *It Had To Be You* is the newest from Beverly Bird, a suspenseful tale of a meant-to-be love. Sara Orwig takes us WAY OUT WEST to meet a *Galahad in Blue Jeans.* Now there's a title that says it all! Finally, look for Barbara Ankrum's *I'll Remember You,* our TRY TO REMEMBER title.

Enjoy them all—and don't forget to come back again next month, because we plan to start off a very happy new year right here in Silhouette Intimate Moments, where the best and most exciting romances are always to be found.

Enjoy!

Leslie J. Wainger
Executive Senior Editor

Please address questions and book requests to:
Silhouette Reader Service
U.S.: 3010 Walden Ave., P.O. Box 1325, Buffalo, NY 14269
Canadian: P.O. Box 609, Fort Erie, Ont. L2A 5X3

IT HAD TO BE YOU

BEVERLY BIRD

Silhouette®

INTIMATE™ MOMENTS®

Published by Silhouette Books

America's Publisher of Contemporary Romance

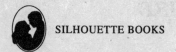

SILHOUETTE BOOKS

RECYCLED PAPER

ISBN 0-373-07970-2

IT HAD TO BE YOU

Copyright © 1999 by Beverly Bird

This edition published by arrangement with Harlequin Books S.A.

® and TM are trademarks of Harlequin Books S.A., used under license.
Trademarks indicated with ® are registered in the United States Patent
and Trademark Office, the Canadian Trade Marks Office and in other
countries.

Visit us at www.romance.net

Printed in U.S.A.

Books by Beverly Bird

Silhouette Intimate Moments

Emeralds in the Dark #3
The Fires of Winter #23
Ride the Wind #139
A Solitary Man #172
*A Man Without Love #630
*A Man Without a Haven #641
*A Man Without a Wife #652
Undercover Cowboy #711
The Marrying Kind #732
Compromising Positions #777
†Loving Mariah #790
†Marrying Jake #802
†Saving Susannah #814
It Had To Be You #970

Silhouette Desire

The Best Reasons #190
Fool's Gold #209
All the Marbles #227
To Love a Stranger #411

*Wounded Warriors
†The Wedding Ring

BEVERLY BIRD

has lived in several places in the United States, but she is currently back where her roots began on an island in New Jersey. Her time is devoted to her family and her writing. She is the author of numerous romance novels, both contemporary and historical. Beverly loves to hear from readers. You can write to her at P.O. Box 350, Brigantine, NJ 08203.

Chapter 1

Shawnalee Collins was having an extraordinarily bad day.

The afternoon was cloudy. A weak sun tried to battle through the haze, then gave up and faded again. A thick humidity hugged Philadelphia, and the sidewalk was still damp from an early rain. Shawna jogged down Second Street, five minutes behind schedule, and the envelope in the pocket of her cardigan felt like a rock.

She slid her hand in to touch it again. The IRS was auditing her. *Her,* a law student. She had made less than twelve thousand dollars last year waitressing in her spare time. How much did they think she could possibly have hidden?

A laugh escaped her, sharp at the edges. Shawna pressed a hand to her mouth.

Now there was an old woman standing on the corner ahead of her blocking Shawna's way. Shawna stepped left to go around her. Something resembling a large rat popped suddenly from behind her bare, veined legs. It was all of five or six pounds, Shawna thought. It was some kind of Chihuahua mix. Its upper lip curled and it growled at her. Shawna quickly stepped back.

"Are you all right?" Shawna asked. Something about the woman was definitely off. She wore only a faded housecoat with short sleeves, though it was barely fifty degrees. The fabric was a dull orange and yellow, but it seemed to take on new life and glow in a beam of watery sunlight that slashed suddenly between two tall buildings on the west side of the street.

The flare of light came and went, giving the woman a surreal look for a minute, like an angel spotlighted in a sea of humanity. She clutched a dirty cardboard box at her midriff. It was strangled in what looked to be a thousand rubber bands.

The woman didn't answer. The dog growled again.

Shawna was a farm girl, born and bred. There was more than one way to skin a cat—or a mongrel, as the case might be. She hunkered down in front of the animal. "Hi, baby." She extended a hand. "Easy now, okay? I'm going to stand up nice and slowly, then I'm going to scoot around you. If you don't let me by, I'm going to be *really* late for work."

"Wait. Don't go yet."

Shawna looked up. The woman was focusing on her now. "I beg your pardon?"

"Don't go. I've been waiting for you."

Shawna stood slowly. "Do I know you?"

"You'll remember me."

"From where?"

"Here. Right here." The woman spoke now with conviction. Shawna didn't share it. She looked around, hoping the woman might be speaking to someone else. No such luck.

Shawna tried to step around her again. The Chihuahua-thing barked crazily.

"Please," the old woman said. "You're the right one. And I can't wait much longer."

"For *what?*"

"Here," the woman said. "It's everything I have."

Shawna grabbed the box as it punched into her stomach. The woman took her wrist. Her skin felt as dry as dust.

Shawna found a leash looped around her own hand—and the dog was at the other end of it. An unpleasant odor wafted up from the box—musty yet somehow pungent, like an old, boarded-up potting shed.

"Wait!" she protested. But the woman was already wading into traffic, crossing the street. Shawna winced as horns blared and at least one set of brakes screamed. Then the woman was gone, disappearing into the chaos as though she had never been.

The dog began yipping excitedly. Shawna glanced down at it helplessly.

She had to tie it someplace. She had to go to work.

A parking meter showed possibilities. Shawna moved that way, then realized that she was dragging the dog. It had squatted down to sit in protest, but it offered pathetically little resistance. Four pounds, Shawna decided, not even five.

"Come on, come on." She scooped it up with one hand. It snarled and bit her.

Shawna cried out and dropped the dog. It yelped

as it hit the pavement, then it scrambled to its feet again to look up at her accusingly.

Shawna glanced at her watch again. It was 3:15. She was so very late now, and all because of the IRS, a woman and a dog.

"Having trouble, lady? Can I help?"

Shawna spun at the sound of the voice behind her. A young man—in his late teens, maybe his early twenties—crossed his arms over his chest and cocked one hip at her. He had long dark hair, parted in the middle. He wore a nose ring and the kind of jeans that were so horribly large on him, they defied the law of gravity to stay up.

Salvation had never looked so sweet.

"Here, you can take this stuff. That lady—" Shawna turned to point, dragging the dog by the leash again as she raised her arm. But, of course, the old woman was long gone. "Anyway, she'll be right back for it all."

"She say that?"

Shawna frowned. The woman hadn't, actually.

A headache was building behind her eyes, the kind that pumped heat with each beat of her heart. And she didn't have time to explain. The Chihuahua was slinking around her legs now, darting here, wriggling there. The leash was becoming wrapped around her ankles. Shawna bent to unwrap it. Her headache squirted hot pain into her skull.

She straightened again. "Look—" Then the boy hit her.

The blow was stunning. It caught her near her left temple, and her headache exploded into red stars. She cried out in disbelief and stumbled backward. She dropped the leash. "Hey! What—"

He shoved her with both hands this time. Shawna pinwheeled one arm for balance, still clutching the box with her other. The dog began barking madly. Shawna's legs tangled as she tried to avoid stepping on it and she went down hard.

The back of her head cracked against the pavement. She heard a sound like a muffled gunshot inside her skull, and pain ricocheted through every inch of her brain.

She was being mugged! Nine years in Philadelphia, and it was finally happening.

Shawna tried to sit up. Her heart was galloping, and astonishment had her breath falling short. The kid was trying to grab the old woman's cardboard box.

Righteous anger raced up from the core of her. She'd been *entrusted* with the box. She was *not* going to give it up. Shawna held on to it and screamed.

Bystanders were gathering, standing around them and gaping. The man—boy, he was barely more than a boy—finally twisted the musty box from her hands. He began running. Shawna watched him leap off his feet to pump the thing triumphantly at the sky.

"Somebody stop him!"

And somebody tried to.

The man came from behind her. Shawna had a flashing impression of black out of the corner of her left eye. He wore a dark overcoat, and she got a glimpse of thick black hair and broad, stubborn shoulders. He was closing in on the boy. Shawna tried to get to her feet and got as far as her knees before she fainted. The red that kept dancing around the edges of her vision turned suddenly black and thick as molasses. She gave a sigh and decided it wasn't worth fighting. She eased down onto the sidewalk as the world went dark.

Voices brought her back first, the kind of excited conversation that happened at the unexpected. Then she smelled something appealing, something warm and spicy that made her want to smile.

Shawna turned into it with another sigh. It was all things good, she thought, a homecoming. She rubbed her cheek against cool wool. Then she felt hands in her hair. They spasmed, gripping her skull.

That hurt.

She opened her eyes. Her nose was pressed to a black overcoat. The man, she thought. The one who had run after that boy.

"Hey, lady, are you all right?" His voice was deep, vaguely husky, with a rough edge to it. Unused was the impression that came to her mind.

"Mmm. Probably."

His hands moved down to her shoulders and he eased her back. Shawna still felt dizzy. Good enough reason, she thought, to take two handfuls of his coat and hold on.

Shawna finally looked up at the man, and her breath stopped. He was…beautiful.

He had blue eyes, the color of the sky in the morning back on the farm, that deep indigo of night giving way to dawn. His face was craggy—dimples had given way to creases—and his jaw was hard. There was a tiny thread of gray through the black at his left temple.

He put his hands over hers. He freed them from his coat with careful deliberation, seeming intent on pulling away from her now that she was conscious. The warm care in his touch seemed a dichotomy.

"Who are you?" Shawna murmured. There was something about him, something visceral that tugged at her deeply. It was a sense of familiarity, she thought.

He dropped her hands and got to his feet without answering. "You probably have a concussion. You cracked your head hard enough that I heard it halfway down the block."

Shawna pressed a hand to the back of her head, then took it away when pain rushed to the spot with a fresh beat. "Actually, the headache started first."

"Let's see if you can stand. Did you hurt anything else?"

"I don't think so." Shawna put her hand in his again. He tugged her to her feet, and she swayed a little.

"Easy." He caught her shoulders, then quickly let her go.

"I'm fine. Thank you." He was stepping away from her. *Don't go. Don't go yet.* "Thanks for doing something."

"I got your things back." He went as far as a parking meter and picked up the musty, banded box.

It was too much. Shawna laughed. It came upon her suddenly, rolling waves of it that made her hiccup and made her eyes tear. The stranger watched her, those blue eyes narrowing.

"What's funny?" he asked finally.

"That woman never came back."

His expression went even harder. "What woman?"

"The one who gave me this." She took the box back. "And the dog." The Chihuahua was finally tied to the parking meter beyond the stranger's left shoulder. It had laid down now, front paws crossed over each other as though the skinny little beast was a bored, well-bred debutante.

Shawna looked back at the stranger. "Didn't you see her? She asked me to hold onto it—the dog and the box. I was going to tie the dog right there, but it bit me. And then that boy came along, that kid, and he *hit* me. Pow! Just like that. I couldn't believe it. I saw you out of the corner of my eye—"

"Ma'am?"

Shawna turned too sharply, and dizziness swam over her again. This time the voice belonged to a cop.

"Can you give us a statement now?" he said.

"I didn't see everything. I was out cold. But he saw everything. He caught him." She thrust a thumb over her shoulder.

"Who?"

"This man." Shawna pivoted again.

He was gone.

She searched the dissipating crowd. There was no sign of him now. She looked down at the box she still held, and her brows drew together.

She looked up again and inhaled deeply. She could still smell it, that scent that had clung to his overcoat…but then that was gone, too.

"We really need a statement now," the cop said again.

"I don't have time." Still, Shawna didn't move. Where had he gone?

"Ma'am—"

"I've got to go. Look, I work at Claire's on South Street. It's the place with the red-striped awnings. Just come there. I'll take a break and tell you anything you want to know.''

"You really ought to see a doctor—''

"I will. Later. I promise.'' In a pig's eye. She wanted this experience over with and behind her.

Shawna moved away, hurrying.

"Hey, you forgot your dog!''

She turned to run backward. "It's not my dog!''

That, however, was a moot point. Someone had untied the little beast from the parking meter and it chased after her. It reached her and jumped against her shins, yapping, possibly the ugliest little creature she had ever seen. Her finger still hurt where it had bitten her. And that stranger was gone as though…well, as though she had imagined him.

But he'd *been* here. Hadn't he? Then again, she did have one wild headache.

She'd never even caught his name.

The pain in her head seemed to shimmy and spread. The dog barked and cavorted in circles around her legs. And somehow, ridiculously, Shawna still held the box.

She sat abruptly on the curb and let herself cry.

Gabriel Marsden watched her from his fourth-floor apartment window. He knew the exact moment when she looked around and realized that he had gone.

Correction, he thought—he'd run, before the lunacy of what he had done could start throwing off repercussions. Like cops talking to him, asking questions, recognizing his face.

He watched her leave the scene abruptly, with a short, exasperated wave of her left hand. No ring there. You've got no business noticing that. But he

had, as soon as she'd dug her fingers into his coat—
the coat he still wore because he had not even paused
to remove it on his way to the window.

She began hurrying down Second now. She took a
few steps, then she turned to run backward, shouting
something. Some helpful hanger-on thought to make
sure she didn't forget her dog. He watched as the
animal—an atrociously ugly little thing—began yapping around her ankles. Then he finally turned away
from the window. He had work to do.

Still, a mental image of that moment when she had
first looked up at him kept flicking on and off in his
brain. Like a TV losing reception only to snap back
into focus. She brought to mind sunflowers. It was all
that golden hair. It wasn't long particularly, but more
shoulder-length. He'd found his hands in it, checking
for blood or lumps or whatever other injury she might
have sustained, so he knew there was a lot of it. And
he knew that it smelled like a meadow in spring. Like
sunflowers bending beneath a hot summer sun.

Almost unconsciously he brought his hand up to
find that her scent still lingered there. Gabriel went
abruptly to the bathroom sink and washed it away.

When he returned to the window, she was still
down there, sitting on the curb. The dog was beside
her, looking at her now with an expectant wag of its
long, skinny tail. She raked a hand through all that
golden hair, and it fell smoothly back into place. She
got to her feet and began to walk away.

The dog followed.

She stopped once, shooing it away. It didn't go.
She sighed and picked it up. It rode on her hip, its
short legs dangling, tucked under her free arm. In her
other, she still held that box.

Gabriel watched until she disappeared. The regret he'd felt when he'd first left her had faded. In its place was an almost poignant sadness that surprised him.

She'd blasted through a few moments of his life like a shooting star, bright and laughing. And now she was gone.

He knew it was all for the better.

Chapter 2

Shawna woke the next morning with a crick in her neck. The alarm *beep-beep-beeped* with tinny, ear-splitting suddenness. She forgot—as she always did—exactly where she had pushed the coffee table last night to get it out of the way. She jumped off the sofa and moved blindly across the living room to turn the sound off, and her shin connected smartly with a corner of the table.

"Oh, damn. Ouch, ouch, ouch." She hopped on one foot to the antique sideboard they used for an entertainment center. She found the clock and flattened her palm against the top of it with a hard smack.

"Can't you ever get to that thing within the first five minutes after it goes off?" Her roommate appeared in the hallway that led to the bedroom. They swapped the bedroom on a monthly basis. This was Katie's term for privacy and comfort.

Shawna straightened from the sideboard with a throaty sigh. "I need coffee."

Katie headed for the kitchen, a sliver of space behind the breakfast bar. She moved about comfortably and competently. "I'll make it."

Shawna waited without argument while Katie brewed and puttered, then she accepted the cup Katie passed across the bar. Shawna sipped. Ah, it was good.

Katie yawned and brought eggs from the refrigerator. "What are your plans for today?"

Shawna groaned. The IRS, she remembered. What was she supposed to do about *that?* And the stranger. Just...gone. But there was a tender knot at the back of her cranium that told her she hadn't imagined it all.

Shawna put her empty mug in the sink and turned away without answering. She got as far as the hallway before Katie stopped her again.

"We can't keep that dog. Don't even think it."

Shawna looked at her feet. As had pretty much been the case ever since she'd brought her home yesterday, the Chihuahua was there.

Shawna had named her Belle. She had to call her something until she could get her back to her rightful owner.

"Our landlady is going to have a coronary when she finds out that we're harboring an animal in here," Katie said.

"*If* our landlady finds out, she *might* have a coronary." Shawna didn't believe in inviting trouble. If you expected the worst, then it would find you sure enough. She *always* looked on the bright side.

So how had she gotten into this mess? The IRS. A

dog she wasn't supposed to have. And a strange-looking box that was smelling up the coffee table.

Shawna wondered again if something had died in there. She'd considered finding out, but the box wasn't hers to open, and sometimes it was just better not to know.

"I'll take the dog back to that corner and see if the woman turns up." In other words, Shawna thought, she would fix one problem at a time.

Katie ran her tongue over her teeth. "I'll come with you. Two sets of eyes have got to be better than one."

Which said a lot about Katie's feelings for the dog, Shawna thought. Like her own, Katie's life was one of too many things to do and not enough hours to do them all in. That she would cough up a precious hour or two to hunt down Belle's owner spoke volumes.

"Give me ten minutes," Shawna said. "Then we'll go look for an odd, old woman in a faded housecoat."

Six blocks away, Gabriel drank some of his own muddy, tepid coffee and closed his eyes in exhaustion. And he saw her again. Why couldn't he get her out of his mind?

In a year, he had never once closed his eyes to find himself haunted by images of Julie, either dead or alive. But everything he remembered about the woman from the mugging had been working on his nerve endings all night, teasing them like a feather. He found himself reliving the scent of her hair, the feel of her against his side when he had held her. And her laughter—bright, vital, happy laughter. As if to say, Life's a bowl of cherries so I'll just toss out this one worm then it won't be there anymore.

She'd been mugged—and then she had laughed.

He wanted—needed—to concentrate on Julie. What he'd found himself doing, instead, was becoming vaguely aroused by thoughts of a woman he was never going to see again. Like a teenager. Like twenty years had fallen away, and he was a randy kid again of sixteen. Maybe, he thought, he was finally losing his mind.

Gabriel placed his cup on the little table that held a coffeemaker and a hot plate. He scrubbed his hands over his unshaven face. The files on the card table he used for a desk seemed to reproach him. He ignored their silent voice.

He needed to eat, he decided. The idea came to him suddenly, and it had a strong appeal. He'd get out of this cramped, confining apartment for a while. He'd have a decent breakfast somewhere, then he would indulge in a long stretch of sleep. If he took a break, if he got away from all this accumulated evidence for a while, maybe something would snap into place for him when he came back.

And maybe *she* would be gone from his thoughts.

Gabriel grabbed his coat from the closet and smelled sunflowers. He ignored them.

He went downstairs. The city stirred but was only just waking. Spring teased the air. The sun was painfully clear in a pale, cloudless sky.

First he would find a pay phone, Gabriel decided.

One would imagine that after six months in Philadelphia, he would have pegged each and every public telephone in his immediate neighborhood. It was not that easy. Gabriel preferred not to use the same one twice. On the day six months ago when his Mercedes had exploded into small, bite-size pieces, he had stopped taking chances.

So he walked. And he walked. Then he hailed a cab to take him a short distance, and finally he walked some more. With each step, the TV in his mind—the one with the blond—kept flicking on and off.

She'd had brown eyes. Not mellow or golden, he thought, but very dark, the kind that usually gave away a brunette who colored her hair. Gabriel would have bet a thousand dollars that this woman's hair color was natural. He was reasonably well versed in such things, having gone through a rainbow of shades with Julie. And he didn't think this woman's particular color could be captured in any bottle.

He finally found a new telephone booth and he pushed her from his mind yet again. He shoveled in a handful of change, pushed buttons, waited. Then he pushed more buttons, this time a code. There was a computer in Dayton, in a storeroom Bobby Gandy had rented for him there, and it spewed forth the phone messages that were pertinent to his investigation.

Bobby was a detective with the NYPD. He'd been Gabriel's partner before he had retired from the force. Bobby had been the one to tell him of the time frame the New York district attorney was stubbornly standing by, a time frame that was blatantly wrong. The D.A. put Julie's death at 9:05 on that Saturday night. But Gabriel knew beyond a doubt that Julie had not died at 9:05. His wife had not even died at 9:10, or at 9:20. Because she had been in their living room with him at 9:30.

He'd told Bobby so, and Bobby had officially passed the information along. Still, there had been no response from the district attorney. The New York authorities had arrested a man who had an alibi from nine-thirty on, but they were barging ahead with the trial, anyway.

Why?

Gabriel didn't know. But he'd made it his mission these last six months to find out.

This week, there was only one message. Gabriel listened to it and groaned, a raw sound, on the edge. The lab had released the DNA results. The skin cells and blood found beneath the fingernails of Julie's right hand were those of her friend's ex-husband, John Thomas Stern—an egocentric Broadway producer who sometimes played at being a director—the man the D.A. had accused of the crimes.

How could it be?

Talia Stern had been killed right beside Julie. And as conventional wisdom had it, wasn't it usually the spouse?

Not this time. Damn it, Gabriel thought. It was something else—another piece—that just didn't add up.

Bobby finished his message with a plea for sanity. "Come on, pal. Let it go. There's your answer. The old guy really did it. Give it up and come on home."

If he went back to New York, would the attempts on his life stop? Gabriel didn't think so.

He made one last call to the telephone company in Ohio. He used recording options to terminate service to the computer there. Tomorrow Reynold Austin would have a line in Kentucky turned on. Reynold was the only other man who knew he was alive.

Gabriel's stomach rumbled.

He began retracing his steps to his own neighborhood, his stride faster now. He knew where a diner was, had passed it a hundred times before on his search for pay phones, a place with red-striped awnings overhanging a bustling street. He'd never gone inside—he went out as little as possible—but he'd noticed it. He cut north on Second and approached Bainbridge, planning to cross over it toward South—and then he stopped cold.

She was standing on the corner.

Not her, Gabriel thought immediately. It couldn't possibly be the woman he had met yesterday. Her image, that quicksilver, laughing, golden-haired image, was haunting him.

That woman yesterday had been dressed nearly all in white—slacks, sneakers, a sweater. This one wore jeans that seemed as close to her skin as morning dew settling over grass. She wore a blue cotton shirt. As he stared, a breeze stirred up and rippled the cotton over her skin like a lover's touch. She was tall, with an agile, loose-limbed grace.

All legs. Golden hair. She scanned the street slowly, glancing left to right. Then right to left again. Looking for someone, he thought. She wore dark, wraparound sunglasses. He couldn't see her eyes. But he finally registered that she was holding that ugly little dog.

Turn around. Go back. If she shifted a little more to her right, she would spot him.

It occurred to him too late. She turned.

Gabriel felt their eyes connect. It was an electric pulse shooting through him. She reached up and snatched off her sunglasses. Her eyes widened—dark brown eyes. Then she gave a delighted smile that seemed to come up from her soul.

Go to her. Gabriel felt an overpowering need to cross the street, to join her on the other corner. Because there was something easy about her that would soothe every tortured memory in his soul. There was something bright in her that would light his way home.

He knew it as surely as he knew that the longer he stood here, the more he was in danger. And still he remained, rooted to the cement.

She spoke. Not to him, but to the woman beside her.

"It's him."

"Who?" Katie frowned, looking around. "I thought we were watching for an old woman."

Shawna finally dragged her gaze from the stranger. "The man from the mugging! I told you about him. The one who got back the box and the dog."

"Where?"

Shawna inclined her head hard, several times, in the direction of the opposite corner. Then she followed Katie's gaze fast. Because the last time she'd turned her back on him, he'd disappeared.

He was still there. Just standing there. Watching her.

He wore the same black coat. She could still feel its incredible softness between her fingers, against her cheek, as though a whole day hadn't passed. Shawna took a step toward him. She moved without conscious awareness of doing so, but the need to go to him was seductive and strong.

Who are you? Why did you come back here? What were the odds? Some things just fought logic. And when that happened, Shawna knew, you had to look for a higher plan.

"What are you doing?" Katie grabbed her arm to stop her.

"I need to talk to him."

"Him? Are you out of your mind? Are you sure *he* didn't mug you? Shawna, for God's sake, look at him."

Shawna did, still half expecting that he might have vanished again. But he hadn't.

"He looks like he hasn't shaved in a week. He probably stole the coat. His jeans are wrinkled. Maybe he slept in them."

All Shawna saw was that he was moving backward now, away from her.

She wasn't going to lose this chance to find out who he was. He was here. She hadn't imagined him. Though Katie made another swipe for her sleeve, Shawna stepped quickly clear.

Gabriel finally found his voice when she was no more than three yards from him, moving dangerously through the traffic that whipped blindly around the corner. She still held her glasses in one hand, and the dog.

"*Stop.*"

Shawna did, startled. "What?"

"Leave me alone."

"But I—"

"For your own sake, just stay the hell away from me."

A car horn blared at her, warning her out of the way. Shawna jumped up onto the curb.

He didn't let her answer, didn't dare. Because if she got close enough in the process, he would catch the scent of her again. *Sunflowers.*

She was trouble. She was dangerous to everything he was and everything he needed to be. Already, without even knowing her name or who she was, she'd distracted him from his mission time and again last night.

Gabriel turned away.

"Wait!" she cried. "Just *wait* a minute! I want to talk to you!"

No can do, lady. He was acting crazy. He knew that. But it was self-preservation, and it was strong.

Gabriel ran.

Chapter 3

By the time Shawna got to the diner to start her shift, nerves were featherlight and twitchy in the pit of her stomach. She couldn't believe any of this was happening to her.

She still had the box. She still had the dog. What she didn't have was a dark-haired, blue-eyed stranger—or even his name—because when he'd spotted her on that corner again, he'd fled as though all the hounds of hell had been on his tail.

Actually, Shawna thought, he'd fled as though *she* was a hound from hell.

"Feeling better?" Katie took a break just as Shawna began her shift. They met in the kitchen as Shawna hung her sweater on a peg on the wall.

Shawna groaned.

"Well, I did our post office run this morning on my way here. I've got more bad news." Katie pulled an envelope from the pocket of her tidy kitchen whites.

Shawna stared at the envelope. *Another* envelope? Plain, no stamp—the IRS was apparently above such trivia—with condensed black letters in the upper left-hand corner. She snatched it from Katie's hand, tore it open, and read fast.

Katie regarded her sadly. "Look, I know an accountant—"

Shawna's jaw dropped. "They changed their mind."

"The IRS doesn't change its mind."

"They do. They did. They made a mistake."

Katie took the letter skeptically. "They never make mistakes. Did God ever say, oops, sorry, didn't mean to flood the Midwest?" But Katie's face changed as she read. Her brows drew together, then her eyes widened. "This is incredible."

Shawna laughed. "That first notice was supposed to go to a different social security number, one digit different from mine. They're letting me off the hook."

Shawna took the letter back. She slid it into her back pocket. Then she took a clean, folded apron from beneath the dish bar and headed for the dining room to start her shift.

In a matter of hours her luck had literally veered. It had gone from miserable—she still had the lump on her head to prove that—into the realm of uncanny.

Shawna left the diner through the back door at midnight, the IRS letter in one pocket, a fifty-dollar bill she'd found on the floor in the other. She stood on the stoop for a moment, hugging herself in the chill air.

Something very, very odd was going on here.

She thought of the phone call she'd gotten from Katie at half past eight, when her roommate had gotten home. There'd been a message on their machine from Culligan, Frost and Myars, the personal-injury law firm in Philadelphia. They wanted her to come in for an interview.

Not *that* surprising, she told herself. Her grades were top-notch. It had taken her nine years to get through college and law school not because she had struggled academically, but because she'd had to work her tail off to pay the rent and fill those financial gaps her student loans hadn't covered. So Culligan was culling the top of the class. She'd had half a dozen other offers from half a dozen lesser-known firms in the last month alone. Shawna would have to make a choice soon—she took the bar exam next week.

It was the timing of this call that drew her skin tighter. And, of course, the prestige of Culligan. She hadn't graduated first in her class—there'd been no time for that kind of dedication. And Culligan could only be expected to take the very best.

Katie had also said that their animal-phobic landlord had called. She was forgiving half the month's rent for a persistent problem with the bathtub that couldn't be easily fixed. Oh, and by the way, did they have a dog in their apartment? Someone had heard it barking. Their lease said no pets. Get rid of it by the end of the month, please.

Shawna took the steps to the street slowly. An idea

was forming—spooky certainly—but it had a certain chronological sense to it, she decided.

Ten minutes later she found herself standing in the same spot where she'd awakened after the mugging. She thought whimsically that she could still feel that stranger here. Who was he? She wanted to know why he had run from her. She wanted to know what it was about him that had kicked off such a chain reaction of good fortune. Because it was *him*. It had something to do with the stranger. She was sure of it.

Shawna wasn't a lucky woman. She wasn't *unlucky* exactly, and she would never complain. But there had been precious few gift horses in her lifetime.

The only unusual thing that had happened to her lately was the mugging, she reflected. That had involved four variables. The woman, the stranger, the box and the dog. The woman was gone. The dog had bitten her. The box smelled. And the stranger had run from her. But the stranger had turned up a second time, and she had only encountered him *then* because she'd been trying to return the box and the dog to the woman.

It was all connected. Somehow.

Shawna opened her eyes slowly, contemplating everything. And then she saw him again.

Across the intersection and about ten feet down the block. The stranger seemed to notice her as well. He turned sharply and began heading back the other way. Shawna's eyes widened. Her pulse went from zero to sixty in the time it took for her to breathe. He was *here*. He was back on this same street corner. At a quarter past midnight?

"No. Oh, no, you don't. Not this time." Shawna broke into a jog as he began to run again.

This time she wasn't wearing boots as she had been that morning. She'd thought about catching up to him then, but in heels, and with the dog, half a block of trying had made the idea seem ludicrous. This time she sprinted.

He never looked back over his shoulder, but he must have sensed her behind him. He picked up speed, his stride lengthening. Shawna moved faster.

"Hey!" she called out. "Just *wait* a minute! *Hold…on!*" Her voice rang out over the subdued midnight hush of the street.

He stopped.

He did it so suddenly she almost ran into him. Any triumph she might have felt at catching up with him was mitigated by the fact that she had to lean against a parking meter, gasping for breath.

"I'm sorry," he said. "Do I know you?"

Shawna straightened again hard and fast.

Uncertainty shivered up her spine. She felt the fierce red of embarrassment heat her skin. But she looked into his eyes, and she knew she'd recognize him anywhere.

She reached out quickly to trace a finger along his clenched hand. "Are you real?"

He pulled back from her touch. *"What?"*

He was definitely flesh and blood, she thought. In all honesty she'd begun to wonder, what with the way he kept at a distance, letting her see him but not letting her get too close…evading her. And with the way he'd changed her luck.

"Please." Her breath was still unsteady. "I need to understand what's going on."

"Nothing's going on." His tone was short. "You're crazy."

"Why are you running from me?"

"Because you keep chasing me."

"I do not." She pulled herself back, stung, then she relaxed a little. "Look, there's obviously a higher plan to all this. We just need to explore it."

A higher plan? Gabriel looked into those depthless brown eyes and felt his head spin. She meant it, he realized.

He opened his mouth, intending to put her off somehow. What he had allowed to happen here was a mistake of magnificent proportions—worse even than yesterday when some knee-jerk reaction had made him take off after her mugger. Now he was standing on an open street talking to her.

But what he'd intended to say didn't come out. "I never caught your name."

Shawna blinked, surprised, then she seized the opportunity. "Shawnalee Collins. Shawn's my dad's name. I have four older sisters. My parents didn't have any boys until after I came along, then they had two. But I think my father gave up hoping for a namesake and he used me just in case." She knew she was babbling. But she felt oddly compelled to tell him as much about herself as possible in whatever time he'd give her. To establish a link. Something substantial, so he couldn't disappear again. "What's yours?"

He looked dazed. "My what?"

"Your *name*."

"Oh. It doesn't matter." He started to move away again.

"*Wait!*" She wasn't sure she had the stamina—or the lack of pride—to run after him again. But this time he didn't go. He just looked tired.

"Look, I don't care about your family history. You have to leave me alone."

Shawna reacted with a flinch, before her mind fully registered the cut of his words. His stance was restless now, edgy. "You mean something to my life," she said quickly. She lifted her hands, let them fall. "I haven't figured it out yet. But it adds up, if you take it from the beginning. It was all so strange, the way I ended up being on this corner so that kid could mug me in the first place. I shouldn't have been here, you know. If everything had been going along normally, I would have passed by here a good five minutes earlier. But the IRS—well, that's a different matter entirely. The point is, I got mugged, and then you came along, out of nowhere. Then, this morning, there you were *again*. And now—this. Here we are, one more time. Something's going on here. What? Why did we meet here again?"

"Because I was looking for you, damn it!"

He'd shouted to get his own voice into the flow of her words.

Shawna went still. Her eyes widened. Then she smiled.

"Well, there you have it. I mean, why would you do that? Why would you be out here looking for me at midnight? You don't even know me."

This was crazy, he thought. She was nuts.

She laughed again, that clean, happy sound. She was delightful.

It was, of course, why he'd come back downstairs when he couldn't sleep again. It was the flash of light and pure emotion that was her, rushing through his dark and urgent world. He hadn't expected to find her. He'd been indulging in…what? Sad sentimentality, he decided, maudlin self-pity for the bizarre turn his life had taken.

It was unlike him, but he'd been in a wallowing mood. It had seemed safe enough to indulge himself at midnight. What were the odds of her turning up a *third* time, in the middle of the night?

"We don't have a connection," he said, trying to be sane. Then he suddenly thought of a way to end this, to curtail something that should never have started in the first place. He would simply tell her his secret. Not all of it. Just enough to make her understand why she had to go away. "Let's get a cup of coffee."

He watched her eyes widen even more. With surprise, innocence, glee. *No one* could be that guileless, he decided.

She began walking, then she looked quickly over her shoulder to make sure he was still with her. Gabriel felt a vague urge to smile, but he beat it. He rubbed a headache out of his forehead instead.

He fell into step beside her.

"Someplace quiet," he cautioned. "Someplace dark."

She stopped suddenly and grabbed his left hand. As he had the first time she had so unexpectedly touched him, Gabriel pulled it away fast. "What are you doing?"

"Are you married?"

"Where did you get *that* from?"

"From someplace quiet and dark."

He understood the leap and her logic. Too easily, he thought, and that shook him a little. Then something sharp and vicious drove through his soul. "No. My wife's dead."

Shawna took breath in sharply. "I'm sorry."

"You didn't know."

She was looking at his right hand now. There *was* a ring there. A plain gold band that caught the light of a street lamp and seemed to take on life of its own. It was a tangible reminder of what he must do, what he had to do, for Julie. He would not take it off until this was over…or he would die wearing it.

The very real probability of the latter brought him back to his senses. A cold breeze kicked up at the same moment, and it seemed to sweep his muggy and brooding mood away. He got sane. What the hell was he thinking?

"Look, this negates the need for that coffee. All you really need to know is that my wife—" How to say it, Gabriel wondered, without the pain and the fear and the disbelief? He broke off, and Shawna marched on.

"Stop," he said sharply. "Damn it, come back here."

"No, you're right. We need to talk."

"Shawnalee—"

"Drop the Lee. Everyone else does."

She caught his hand again to urge him on. She touched easily, he thought, without restraint or caution, just the way she gave in to her feelings. This time he felt the heat beneath her skin, fast and fleeting.

A connection? A mistake. But he let her pull him into a coffee shop on the corner.

A little bell sounded obnoxiously over their heads when they stepped inside. There were real leather stools and cheap vinyl banquettes, he noticed, with overhead fans blowing around stale and greasy air. It was a place that had probably gone through a variety of owners over the years. Some had put their profits right back into the business; others had reamed it for every ounce of cash it would provide.

There was a woman at the end of the counter, with tinted black hair, wearing too-tight jeans. A soft-drink emblem covered most of the wall in front of her, its red fading.

Shawna slid into the first booth. Gabriel sat across from her. He ordered two mugs of coffee when the waitress approached from the counter.

"Do you want anything else? Something to eat?" He'd forgotten how to do this, he realized, how to be sociable.

Shawna's stomach was rolling—with expectancy and something jittery and delicious. She shook her head and grinned at him.

"Stop looking at me like that."

Her smile went to a frown of concern. "How am I looking?"

"Like I'm the best thing that's happened to you all day."

"I'm still trying to figure out *what* you are."

That makes two of us, lady. He was trying to figure out what it was about her that had urged him to let her in even this far. He had not had coffee with anyone in six months. He had not spoken more than a sentence or two to anyone in all that time.

He rubbed his throat absently as the waitress brought their coffee. He watched Shawna pour in cream, then too much sugar. He wondered where to begin, how to end this. Then she chattered on.

"You know, even with all the coincidence in meeting you yesterday, I might have...I don't know, overlooked all that.'' She waved her spoon in a little circular motion. A droplet of coffee flew off and he wiped it absently from the table with his finger. ''But the thing is, I saw you again today. And then all these good things started happening to me.''

''Good things.''

''It's been like this *rush* of good luck.''

''And you don't believe in luck.''

She looked up from her coffee, startled. ''Of course, I do. You know, people tend to chalk up to luck and coincidence all those things that they just don't understand. And, I might add, these are the same people who troop to their various houses of worship on weekends. So why not just give someone upstairs the credit? Why be coy about it?''

It scared the hell out of him, but he was still following her.

''I mean, just admit it and accept it. Coincidence is the work of something bigger and smarter than we are, pushing us along, trying to nudge us where we're supposed to go. Or to get our attention. I definitely believe that.''

It was as good an explanation as any, Gabriel thought. Still, he said nothing.

''Luck, serendipity—all of it, the work of a higher power. When it starts kicking in, it's important to pay attention.'' She stopped for breath. ''Now, with that in mind, explain why you went to Second and Bainbridge to find me at midnight.''

He had a few answers for that, but he'd already told her all he was going to.

''You *knew* I'd be there, didn't you?''

He scowled. ''I did not.''

''Maybe not consciously. Instinctually.''

He found himself wondering, dazed, if it were possible.

"You know, I was starting to think you were an angel. But then I touched you. And you're definitely here."

Gabriel choked on coffee. "You've been watching too much television."

"Between law school and working full-time and studying for the bar?" She laughed again. "Get serious."

She was a student? She didn't seem that young. Her spark wasn't naiveté, he realized, but a certain kind of determined hope.

"Anyway, what does television have to do with this?"

Gabriel brought himself back. "There's a popular show right now about angels coming to earth." Or at least there had been, six months ago. He hadn't seen a TV since then. "I think the idea is that the people who encounter them can actually touch them."

Her eyes narrowed as she considered this, then she shook her head. "No, you're real. The luck was just to get my attention. You know, just to be very sure that I didn't forget you." She grew thoughtful. "I didn't. And that got me to wandering the streets at midnight."

The way he had been. Something jerked in the area of Gabriel's chest. Then the bell rang over the door, and he came half to his feet, his blood heating, his fists clenched.

It was a woman with blue hair and a cane, dressed to the nines after a night out.

Gabriel settled down again. Something oily filled his stomach. *Why was he doing this?*

Why was he risking his life now, so far into the war he couldn't remember when he hadn't fought it? He'd accepted the deprivation. He'd embraced the lack of human contact these past six months. Now, in the space of two days, he was throwing it to the wind. Because Shawnalee Collins had left him no alternative.

But that was taking the easy way out.

He *wanted* to be here, he realized. God help him, but this woman was like the first spring breeze after an arctic winter. She bewitched him.

Those guileless brown eyes were sharp now, a little narrowed. She glanced at the woman who had just walked in then back at him. "Kind of jumpy, aren't you?"

Gabriel cleared his throat. "I need to get out of here."

"Why? We just got here."

It was what he had come here to tell her, but now the words were gone. *Tell her now. Make her understand why she has to leave you alone.* The gold band on his right hand seemed to glow again in the overhead lights, reminding him, urging him on.

Gabriel stood. He took some bills from his pocket and threw a couple on the table.

"I've got an obligation. I can't be sidetracked from it. And you're sidetracking me." He leaned forward to flatten both his palms on the table. "If you get tangled up with me, you could die. I could die. Is that clear enough?" If he didn't remain focused, careful, on his guard, it could happen. He doubted if Julie's killer knew he was still alive and in Philadelphia, but that could change in a moment if he continued this risky behavior.

Impossibly, her eyes took on a gleam of intrigue.

"I thought when you kept running...I don't know, that you were some kind of underworld spy. Or an assassin. Or—"

"Damn it, this is not a game!" She jumped slightly when he raised his voice. "It's real. It's all those things, and more. I'm trying to protect you. And I don't have time for this right now." He straightened from the table. "I don't have time for you."

Her face paled. He'd hurt her.

Whatever worked.

"But you said you were looking for me," she murmured.

He had been. But now, at last, he'd come to his senses.

"Past tense, lady."

With that Gabriel turned and walked out the door.

Chapter 4

He heard her come to her feet behind him. The overhead bell jangled again when he went outside. Then Gabriel stopped on the threshold, standing as still as stone.

Shawna bumped into him from behind. He shot a hand out to stop her. "Wait."

The man was standing on the far left corner. Maybe it was an ex-cop's instinct that had made Gabriel look that way. Or the sheer triteness of it, he thought, the theatrical edge. The man was leaning against a mailbox, pretending to read a newspaper like he would in a bad play.

Shawna turned back for the door.

"*Not in there.*" They'd be cornered, he thought, dead. He caught her elbow, turned right, out of the doorway, and broke into a jog.

They reached the corner and Gabriel looked back. The guy shoved the newspaper down into the mailbox. Newsprint thrust out from the metal door. The man started across the street, toward them. Gabriel pulled her into an all-out run.

"Is that man *chasing* us?" Shawna gasped.

"Yeah." Gabriel had time for a crazy thought. Now, at last, she would understand why she had to leave him alone.

He waited for her next natural question: Why? Why would a man read a paper on the street in the middle of the night, then chase them?

"Stay with me," she said instead. "I think I can lose him."

Without warning, she jerked sideways, pulling him with her. She led him through another turn, into a narrow, night-dark alley. Here, there was no light at all.

Buildings rose above them like urban cliffs, and the moon was trapped behind them. Shadows pooled around the stoops of apartment buildings, blacker than the night. A cat dozed on top of a trash can. When they ran by, it came to its feet, back bowed and hissing.

It felt like a dream. They whipped around another corner into another adjoining alley, then she made a right and he followed her. The suddenness of the street lamps hurt his eyes when they came out again onto an avenue.

In the next alley, Gabriel stopped her. "Wait a minute. *Wait.* Where are we?"

Shawna pulled breath in and waved at a small, redstriped awning less than halfway down the block. "I work there."

Gabriel thought about the awning of the restaurant

he'd been headed for this morning. Coincidence? For a moment, his breath felt even shorter.

"It's the employee's entrance," she said. "We can scoot right on through the restaurant to the front again. They're open until two."

"Just wait a minute."

Gabriel glanced left, then right. No sign of John Thomas Stern's hoodlum. Not Stern, can't be Stern. But there was no time yet to grapple with the issue of who had sent Mr. Newspaper.

Shawna kept fidgeting, shifting her weight from one foot to the other. She was ready to bolt again. From a very wise sense of fear? he wondered. There was a certain light in her eyes now. Gabriel could see it even in the darkness, and it made him uneasy. "Stand still."

Shawna stopped moving. But it was hard to just *stand.*

Her heart was booming, and each time it did, a rush of adrenaline poured into her blood. She turned a little, only intending to look back the way they had come. But he must have thought she was going to run again, because he planted his hands against the brick on either side of her, trapping her. "I said, *don't move.*"

He didn't touch her. His palms were a good six inches from either side of her head. But it didn't matter. Shawna still caught the spicy, warm scent of him. Something deeply buried inside of her leaped singing to the surface to vibrate just beneath her skin. Suddenly her heart was slamming into her throat.

She looked up into his face. His mouth was flattened into an unhappy line.

Her thoughts tumbled away from the bizarre mess

they seemed to be in, falling into speculation that made her breath catch. Something scurried in the pit of her stomach. She wondered suddenly what it would be like to touch her lips to his, if she would be able to coax that mouth into softness. She wanted to try…badly enough that it shook her.

She looked down the alley again instead, away from him. "Are we safe now?"

"I don't know."

"Then we should—"

"*No.*"

Shawna jumped again at the force in his tone. "Okay, okay."

"No more running. Let me think."

"I said okay."

He paused. She waited.

"Where are we?"

Shawna thought about it. "Half a block off South."

"East or west of Second?"

"West." Her breath was finally steadying. "I take it this has something to do with that obligation you mentioned?"

"Yeah."

"Are you going to tell me what it is now?"

"No. It's none of your business."

He straightened away from her, from the wall. She felt alone when he left her, and for the first time she realized that the temperature had plummeted as the night had deepened. Shawna shivered, and she saw his face change again with a quick grimace. It was almost as though letting go of that hard, grim edge was a conscious effort for him. Like he had forgotten how to be kind.

"Don't be frightened," he said quietly.

Fear wasn't actually the first thing on her mind. He was with her, after all. Her angel. Well, *some* kind of angel. She thought about buying a lottery ticket tomorrow.

"I'm sorry for getting you into this." His next words chilled her. "There's every chance that guy meant to kill me."

Shawna came away from the wall and looked around. "*That* was what all the running was about?" She lifted her hand and pulled an imaginary trigger. "Pow, boom, you're dead?"

"Pow, boom. Come on. I'll walk you home."

Shawna's heart dropped. She didn't want to go home. She wanted to know what was going on here. "Tell me," she said. "*Please* tell me what's happening."

"I can't."

"But I just saved your life!"

"I wouldn't go that far."

Suddenly Gabriel was tired, achingly tired. Six months. *Six months,* and he still had no answers, and now someone knew he was alive and in Philadelphia.

Mr. Newspaper hadn't exactly thrown him off his stride. Gabriel had been seeing the guy for a while now when he *didn't* exist, expecting to find him with every glance out his window. So, in an odd way, his actual appearance was a relief. But Shawnalee Collins was a stunning complication.

She stomped her foot in frustration. In spite of everything, Gabriel felt one corner of his mouth pull into a smile. He rubbed it away. "How far do you live from here?"

"Six blocks." Shawna sighed. "Give or take."

It wouldn't work, he thought. It was too far.

If that guy was still roaming around, they'd never make it. Where the hell was he? Out there somewhere, certainly, trying to pick up their trail again. Gabriel didn't think he would give up yet. So they had to get off the street, and another public place was out of the question. That was what had started this nightmare in the first place.

Gabriel thought of a worst-case scenario. Maybe there was more than one of them. Maybe Mr. Newspaper had a few pals he wouldn't recognize until it was too late.

His place, then.

Protest wrapped itself hard around his muscles, and it hurt. One step inside, and she'd know who he was. It was a miracle she hadn't figured it out already.

But what choice did he have? If he shooed her away now, she'd be in no less danger. If that guy encountered her again, recognized her, she might not get home at all.

His fault. Protest turned to something rancid in his throat. Like it or not, she was his responsibility. For now.

"Take us to Second. You know, by the alleys. However it was that you got us here."

Shawna nodded.

They walked this time. They reached the end of the sidewalk, then they crossed the street into another alley. They came out on Second again, half a block from the corner of Bainbridge. Gabriel took a breath, then took the plunge. "This way."

They went to the corner and stepped through a narrow and dark doorway. Shawna glanced around and felt something hitch near her heart, as though she were on the brink of something huge and life altering. Then again, she thought, she'd felt that way all night.

She looked at him, at his hard and unhappy face, and everything calmed inside her. She let out a sigh, a satisfied sound.

Gabriel had no trouble interpreting it. "Are you out of your mind?"

Shawna shrugged. "Where are we going, exactly?"

"My place."

"You *live* here?" There was something strong-willed and sure about him. That black coat was soft as a whisper and had to have cost dearly. None of it fit with a man who would live in these surroundings.

He glowered at her but didn't answer.

Shawna followed him to the back of a vestibule. There were steps there. As they climbed them, she caught the odor of onions that had long since been fried. In spite of the hour, tinned sounds of television laughter emanated into the stairwell, like the voices of ghosts from another time.

"Watch your step. No one's replaced these light bulbs in all the time I've been here."

"How long is that?"

He looked at her sharply. "You don't give up, do you?"

"I want to understand."

They climbed four floors. At the top was another short corridor with a door at either end. He turned left. Shawna followed, and he inserted various keys into...her eyes widened and she counted.

Four locks?

The door finally swung open. Shawna frowned at him and stepped inside.

Red neon pulsed through the windows from a sign just outside. She turned left, then right. He switched on a light.

The apartment was L-shaped. Tucked back into the short side was a twin bed covered by a plain, green, army-issue blanket. There was a single closed door beside it. The main part of the room was small, with a fireplace against one wall. A sofa with hollowed-out, tired cushions sat beneath a line of windows. A gold hooked rug partially covered the hardwood floor.

And that was where any resemblance to an actual home ended, she thought. The walls were covered with poster boards. There was a card table between the sofa and the fireplace. At least twenty-five manila folders sat on top of it, most of them bulging, some held together with rubber bands. All of them appeared to be labeled.

Photographs were interspersed with the poster boards on the walls. There were a few of a brownstone taken from various angles, then another long line of faces…some of whom she recognized. Shawna's heart kicked once, hard.

Some sort of list was tacked beneath each photo. Shawna stepped closer to one and saw that it was a time line, an itinerary of where that person had been at various times on a day nearly a year ago.

That date. Those faces. She looked back at him warily. Then she turned to a photograph over the fireplace mantel. And it all came together.

The photo was large, the centerpiece of this strange tableau. Shawna had definitely seen *that* face before. She knew the high, slanted cheekbones, the straight fall of ebony hair, the eyes that smoldered and laughed by turn. The woman's face had been all over

America for a while. She'd been a model. Lately she had been creeping up in news broadcasts again because the man who had murdered her was about to go on trial.

Julie Marsden.

My wife's dead.

Shawna's blood went icy, then hot.

"How did your wife die?" Her voice scraped through a throat that suddenly felt too tight. She needed to be sure, *absolutely* sure.

"Hard to say. There were forty-two separate stab wounds. The coroner thinks it was probably the last one, the one to her throat, that killed her. They're all detailed nicely in photographs in that top folder there. I don't think you want to see them."

Shawna felt faint. *What had she stumbled into here?* "You have pictures?"

"I have everything."

"You're...you're..." *Gabriel Marsden.* It was, of course, the only thing that made sense. No wonder she'd thought she knew him. She'd read a few of his books. She'd seen his photo on the jackets. *Gabriel Marsden.*

But Gabriel Marsden was supposed to be dead. She remembered the car bombing. That had made national news for a few straight weeks, too. First the beautiful model had been killed, then her bestselling writer husband had been blasted to heaven.

She spun on him. "You are such a liar!"

"Given all the other sins involved here, that one is relatively minor."

Shawna moved unsteadily to the sofa and flopped down. He sat on the opposite end, keeping his distance. She narrowed her eyes on him.

"Stern's on trial for killing *both* of you. Are you going to let him be convicted while you're walking around saving mugged women?"

"Your mugging wasn't part of the plan." His voice went harsh, then weary. "I won't let it get that far. I'll have the answers before then. I'm going to find out who killed her."

"It was John Thomas Stern."

"No. They have the wrong man."

As suddenly as he had sat, he rose from the sofa again. He paced, Shawna thought, like an animal who was being gnawed by hunger. Or like one haunted by a deep, internal pain. One who thought only only movement could save him.

"It was supposed to have been like a hundred other nights." She realized that he was telling her how it had happened. "Julie wanted to go clubbing. She called Talia Stern. She left for Talia's brownstone at about nine-thirty. And at twelve-thirty a pedestrian found them on Talia's stoop. No club for the girls *that* night."

Shawna flinched at the raw grief in his tone. And there was something else there, too, something she couldn't quite identify. But it was bitter.

"Sometime after the funeral, I started to write about it. To work the grief out of my system. It was the only way I knew how. I started to bury myself in the murder."

Shawna nodded.

"I have a friend with the NYPD. He was my partner, back when I was a cop. He gave me copies of the police files."

The pictures, Shawna thought. That explained how he had come by them.

''That was when I realized that the D.A. was trying to put the deaths at 9:05.'' He stopped pacing. ''Five days before my car went up, Bobby went to•the D.A. with my statement, to tell them that their estimated time of death was wrong. It was too early. At the time they had Julie and Talia being killed, Julie was with me. No one got back to me. Their investigation was headed off in the wrong direction, but nobody seemed to care.''

''You wrote about that. I saw it in the paper.'' She remembered the syndicated series he'd started on the killings, articles that had just been warming up—and stirring things up—when they'd abruptly ended with his ''death.''

''Yeah. I have another buddy—Reynold Austin—who's the editor-in-chief of the *Monitor* in New York. He gave me a platform to purge when that was what I needed, and other papers picked up on the stories. Everyone wanted to hear from me in those weeks, to share the grief and the horror and the gore.''

Shawna nodded, understanding that.

''I wrote about the time of death being wrong, and the next day I pulled over to the side of Fifty-Fourth Street and got out of the car to buy my daily load of newspapers.'' He stopped at the window, looked out, moved on. ''I was maybe ten feet from the curb and *boom*.''

''But people had to have seen that you weren't in the car when it went up!''

''Have you ever seen a car explode?''

''Sure.'' She gave him a sarcastic look.

One corner of his mouth quirked. ''It creates a little chaos.''

''Fire.''

"Flames, sure. And glass—*parts*—flying. People screaming." He remembered turning, stunned, then acting without any conscious thought at all. It had been instinct. Survival instinct. He'd backed up. Two paces. Four. Then he'd turned and run. Knowing that it was time to hide.

In the confusion, apparently no one had noticed him. And not a soul had ever knowingly seen him alive again.

For six months now, he had been living in shadows. Hiding. Trying to figure out who had killed Julie, so he could avenge her death and reclaim his own life. So he could move on.

If he lived that long.

Shawna pressed her fingers to her temples. "The killer blew your car up?"

"That'd be my guess."

"John Thomas Stern was already in jail by then. And he had everything to gain if you let America know he might be the wrong man."

"Mmm."

"*Wow.*" She shot off the sofa to face him.

"Shawna—"

"No, this is really something. My God."

The reality of his situation, of who he was and why that guy had been chasing them earlier, was all beginning to pile together into a full picture. And then there was the amazing realization that *she* was involved, Shawna thought. Someone had chased *her*. Well, clearly, the guy had been chasing Gabriel, but if he had caught up with them, Shawna doubted very much if he would have patted her on the shoulder and told her to go on home.

"What's wrong with Stern's lawyers?" Her mind raced.

Gabriel snarled. "High-priced fools, more concerned with preening for the cameras."

She wasn't going to argue with him on *that*. She had a slew full of her own opinions. "But what can *you* do," she asked, "when you're not even alive?"

She reduced the problem to its simplest terms, Gabriel thought, in the space of a breath. "I have ways."

"Like what?"

"You don't need to know that."

"I'm curious."

No, he thought. No. He had let her in as far as she was going to go.

Then he realized that for the first time in months his jaw didn't hurt from grinding his teeth. His arm didn't ache from clenching his fists. He breathed. The ever-present weight on his chest had eased a little.

She hadn't told him he was crazy.

"I could help you," she said, and he ground his teeth and clenched his hands again.

"No, I'm serious. I could. I'm a lawyer. Well, not yet. Not quite. But I will be next week, when I take the bar exam."

"Unless you can get a job with the New York District Attorney's Office within the next few days, I don't see what good that will do."

"You're missing my point."

"Maybe because it's in the stratosphere."

"Will you just *listen?*"

Gabriel looked at his watch again, then out the window. He wondered if that guy had given up yet so he could get her safely home.

"I'm smart." She said it without pride, catching

his attention again. "I could help you figure this out. How long have you been at it now? It's been nearly a year since the murders. And you haven't gotten anywhere, have you? You got to the bottom of all those other killings, the ones you wrote about in your books, but—"

He interrupted her for the sake of his own sanity. And yes, to defend himself. His pride had taken a small hit. "It's only been six months since I got serious."

Shawna waved a hand, dismissing that. "My point is, you need fresh eyes."

"I'm fine."

"Are you going to write about it? Another book?"

The question broadsided him. He honestly hadn't thought about a book before. It had never been about that. But it was natural curiosity. His works were all true-crime facts laid down under a thin film of dramatic, fictional gauze.

Would he sell Julie's death for a royalty percentage? "If that's the only way America will listen to the truth when I find it. Come on, I'm taking you home."

"Wait. I'm *supposed* to be involved in this!"

Without thinking, he closed the distance between them. He put his hands on her shoulders. Maybe he wanted to shake some sense into her. But whatever his intention might have been, it fled from his mind the moment he touched her.

She was warm, soft. Her lips were slightly parted in surprise, her eyes agitated, and her breath touched his face. He felt the beat of her life, the heat of emotion gathering within her again. Outside of picking her up off the sidewalk yesterday, he hadn't touched another living soul in six months.

Something happened to his throat.

Gabriel took his hands away fast. He turned his back on her.

"It's not serendipity," he said hoarsely. "It's not fate, not coincidence. It's murder." He looked over his shoulder at her again. At last, she seemed to be listening. "John Thomas Stern is in jail for killing my wife. I know something's wrong with the D.A.'s case. When I started publicizing that, someone tried to kill *me*. Stern? Why? Like you said, he's got no motive. No, Shawna, the person who tried to kill me is most likely the person who really killed Julie and Talia, the same person who would receive a death sentence if the truth came out. We're talking *death* here, the ending of life. People fight viciously to save their lives. In the end, it's our one common thread as living things—that urge for survival. It makes animals gnaw off a leg if one of them gets caught in a trap." He turned to face her fully again. "If you got involved in this, you could *stop living*."

"You could stop living, too."

"I know that. But I don't care."

"Of course you do. If you wanted to die, you'd have no conscience. You wouldn't be trying to push me out of this."

"It's a moot point!" he shouted, angry. "We're talking about you!"

Yes, they were, Shawna thought. And she wasn't reaching him. She wasn't even sure she entirely understood the compulsion she felt to be a part of Gabriel's investigation herself.

When that happened, it was best to back off and

think things through. Now that she knew where he lived, she could always find him again once she had sorted her feelings out.

Shawna left him and went to the window. She leaned over the sofa and pulled back one yellowed Venetian blind. It wasn't dirty, but time had been hard on it.

No one on the street below was reading a newspaper. She scanned the few pedestrians and saw nothing amiss. "Let's go."

"You're going to leave now?"

"That's what I said, didn't I?"

She went to the door. She threw back the locks. Gabriel's heart seized.

"Wait, Shawna. Don't do that."

She looked over her shoulder at him. "Why?"

"Let me go first."

"And they said chivalry was dead."

"Do you take any of this seriously?"

"Of course."

Sure, she did, he thought. Fate, karma and higher plans. "Just let me go first."

Shawna stepped away from the door almost too graciously. He opened it a crack, looking out. Her voice floated over his shoulder to him.

"If he *is* out there, we've got a big problem. We're cornered in here."

It occurred to Gabriel every time he opened this door. "Stop thinking so much."

"I can't. I told you. It's in my nature. Do you have a gun?"

That startled him. "No."

"You *don't?*"

"I didn't have time to buy one legitimately before I died."

Gabriel determined that the coast was clear and stepped out into the hall. Shawna followed him, and he locked up again behind her.

"Watch out!"

Gabriel spun back to face the hall. A sizzling flood of rage filled his blood and stained the edges of his vision a dull red. Now, finally, end this. He was ready to kill, to fight.

But no one was there.

Gabriel turned his fury on her. Shawna saw it in his eyes. He was closer to the edge than she'd realized. But she held her ground. "Gotcha."

"Damn it! Damn *you!* This isn't a game! Are you crazy?"

"I was making a point, Gabriel. Get yourself a gun."

All he'd wanted was to finish this. He'd wanted dark, quiet nights in which to concentrate. What he'd somehow gotten instead was a dauntless blonde who had absolutely no respect for the situation, a woman who was ripping through his life, leaving everything overturned in her wake, and smelling vaguely like sunflowers.

And he'd opened the door to let her in.

Gabriel rubbed at his temples, wondering why he was going to bother to explain. She'd be gone soon, within half an hour.

"I can't get a gun now," he said tiredly. "I can't register it. I'm dead. And I don't know who I'm up against. It's someone wealthy, someone with significant resources. Someone hired that guy who was chasing us."

Shawna thought about it. "He could see to it that you were tossed behind bars if you were caught with an unregistered handgun."

"And that would take me out of circulation. It would limit my interference. The D.A. might like that, too. They sure as hell don't want to hear what I have to say."

"You can't risk it."

"No." Now that that was out of the way, he had to get her home. "Think you can make it back down to the street without any more theatrics?"

"Sure." She pushed off the wall and headed for the stairs.

"Why don't I believe that?" He spoke to himself, but she heard him. Shawna glanced over her shoulder at him and smiled.

"Because you're a wise man."

Chapter 5

They stayed on the streets this time, and Gabriel kept his eyes on the pedestrians they passed. No one stirred his ex-cop's antennae. Shawna had stopped at the entrance of an elegant high-rise. He took a few steps without her before he realized he'd left her behind.

Gabriel looked back, his heart kicking. ''Come on. We've got to—''

''I used to dream of something like this.''

Gabriel flicked an impatient glance to his left, another to his right. ''Of what?''

She spread her arms wide. ''Of living in a place like this.''

Gabriel glanced up at glimmering windows climbing into the stars. He *did* live in a place like this. Or he had. In another world, another lifetime, called New York.

''I'd be terribly successful.'' Her voice was soft now and a little surprised, as though she were discovering something she'd forgotten. "I'd come home after a day of making a difference, you know, to the world, or to someone's life. A real public advocate. Then I'd kick off three-hundred-dollar heels—it would have to be casually, as though they didn't mean a thing, because I could afford a hundred more pairs—and I'd pour a glass of very expensive wine and I'd take it to a window overlooking all the city lights. I'd be satisfied." She paused. "That's what brought me to Philadelphia. It's how I thought it would be here."

"Public advocates generally can't afford expensive wine."

"Maybe that was just my pro bono work."

"No man in this scenario?"

"He's waiting for me in the bedroom."

Gabriel laughed. It was a rusty, unused sound that cut through his throat like a razor. He was going to miss this woman.

Shawna shrugged and turned to go, and for the first time he thought he saw a hint of self-consciousness in her expression. There's a layer, he thought, following her. One which, under different circumstances, he would have enjoyed peeling away and peering beneath.

He thought of something she'd said earlier. "If you're taking the bar exam next week, I wouldn't write the dream off yet."

"Whatever." But her tone changed.

"What changed?"

"I lost my rose-colored glasses."

They fell into an easy, simultaneous stride. Gabriel went back to trying to keep an eye on the passers-by. His diligence lasted through maybe eight more steps.

"How about you?" she asked. "What did you dream of?"

Gabriel found himself thinking about it, though he wasn't generally a man given to introspection. He picked things apart—that was his nature, and now it was his chosen career. But he did it with the facts and feelings of other people's lives, not his own.

"I played football," he said finally. "From the time I was about seven all the way through high school."

Some would not have considered it to be an answer, but she made the connection. "You were aggressive."

"I tackled things."

"You still do."

He thought about that. "When they need to be tackled."

"Did you know you'd be a writer?"

"I wanted to be a prosecutor."

She stopped walking again. "*You* wanted to be a *lawyer?*"

He was stung. "What's so surprising about that?"

"It's not, well...noble."

"You think I'm *noble?*"

"Well, you've devoted months of your life to finding Julie's killer."

Something thorny filled his stomach. He didn't answer.

"Did you go to law school?"

Gabriel shook his head. "No money. I became a cop instead."

She began walking again. He went after her and found himself trying to explain.

"I made detective, but there were too many rules.

Too many lines to toe. I wanted to get to the truth, but working within the system seemed to prevent it as often as not. So I finally figured out that the only way I could do what I wanted without getting slapped down—or worse, having a case thrown out of court— was to investigate on my own. When no one would listen to me, I started writing about it. I put the truth out there for everyone to see."

"See?" She seemed satisfied. "You *are* noble."

A couple of hours ago she'd thought he was an angel. He felt compelled to argue with her. "I'm a realist. The system stinks. Human nature can be rotten to the core. And let's keep in mind that none of my books have resulted in a conviction."

They'd reached the end of the block. "They were fiction. Were they intended to convict anyone?"

She did have a way of cutting right to the quick. Gabriel thought about it.

No, he realized. They hadn't been. In very large measure, his books were purely entertainment. They were based on truth, but people wanted diversion, not brutal honesty. "Having failed just takes some of the polish off the apple," he said finally.

Shawna stopped to pick up a discarded candy wrapper. She dropped it into the next trash can they came to. "*You* could take off three-hundred-dollar shoes and stroll casually to a window with a glass of fine wine, knowing you'd made a difference."

She was always looking for the bright side. He wondered how often she found it.

"This is it," she said, stopping once more. "I live here."

Gabriel looked up. And he felt his blood chill.

It wasn't a brownstone, but the building had the

same aged and dignified aura as the place where Julie had been killed. Its stone façade was tired, but once, in another era, it had probably been upscale and elegant.

It brought Gabriel back to reality, hard and fast and not entirely painlessly. It felt like an omen, like something bigger and smarter than himself was whispering warnings in his ear. A higher power? Then, he thought, he would be crazy not to heed it.

"Go on," he said quietly. "Go inside."

Shawna didn't answer. Her silence made him take his gaze from the building and look at her again. Her eyes were dark and bright. She'd tucked that golden hair behind both ears, and she watched him with half a smile.

His voice went a little hoarse. "I mean it. Go inside, Shawna, and don't look back. For your own sake. You've already had a good taste of what this involves."

She nodded. Too easily, he thought.

"It won't work," he said.

"What?" Her eyes widened, all innocence.

"Coming back to my apartment. I won't be there anymore."

For once, she looked honestly horrified. "You'd move because of *me?*"

The sound he made was a ragged breath. Then he heard himself explaining one more time. "Only two people were supposed to know that I'm alive."

"Including me?"

Gabriel winced. "No. You're the third."

"Ah." She grinned a little apologetically, tilting her head to one side.

''Bobby—my detective friend—knows. And so does Reynold.''

''The editor.''

He nodded. ''But they don't know where I am.'' They weren't supposed to.

''*Someone* knows where you are.'' She paused. ''So you're going to leave Philadelphia and disappear again?''

''If I want to stay alive long enough to finish this, I have to.''

''Without telling me where you're going?''

A pain hit his chest. ''Shawna, I *can't.*''

In spite of everything she'd learned at his apartment, she hadn't really believed it would end here. Not now that they'd had a chance to talk. She looked away, biting her lip.

''Don't,'' he said.

She looked at him again sharply. ''Don't what?'' she demanded. ''Don't be sorry?''

It was another new layer, he thought, that fire in her eyes now. She had a temper.

''You *need* me,'' she insisted.

''You're the only one who thinks so.'' He took a breath. ''Go upstairs, Shawna. Take the bar exam next week and climb your way to your penthouse in the sky.''

''I don't—''

He interrupted her again, before he could decide not to. ''You've made a difference.''

''I haven't *done* anything yet!''

But she had.

For a few priceless hours he hadn't been isolated in his own silence, alone. Gabriel realized with a jerk of his heart that he fully expected that something would fall into place for him now—a piece that he hadn't seen before would glare at him when he finally went back to his folders and notes. *This* was the break he'd needed. She was the breath of fresh air.

She took two quick steps in retreat and turned for the door.

Sometimes, she thought, things hurt so badly a person just had to run from them. Strange that this should be one of those things. She hadn't known him long enough to feel so *abandoned*. But the pressure in her chest was building, and she realized, appalled, that what she was feeling was an urge to cry.

He was supposed to have meant more to her life than this, something more than fleeting quicksilver passing through it. The good luck, the coincidence…she'd been so *sure*.

"Shawna, wait—" Gabriel caught her sleeve, stopping her short, surprising himself.

She'd startled him. He hadn't expected her to give up so easily. It wasn't her style—that he already knew. He had a moment to consider it, then to understand that once she passed through that door…she was gone. Really gone this time.

He *would* leave Philadelphia. He had to. And this— whatever this had been with her—would be over.

The need to postpone that was selfish. Snatching back a memory before she disappeared was crazy and indulgent. Gabriel touched her, anyway. He had to.

He put a hand to her cheek, satin smooth, and traced a finger along the line of her jaw. He had not touched another woman in eleven years now. But Julie was gone.

"What?" she whispered.

"Just give me another minute." Self-recriminations already sang in him, but he pulled her into his arms.

Shawna gave a soundless cry. He hoped it was a sound of surprise, because if it was one of protest, he was probably damned. He was somehow convinced that the taste of her, too, would be unique—sunshine, heat and promise. And he had to know.

He wanted to feel again. He wanted to touch again. But it was more than that. It had to be *her*.

When he felt her against him, the hunger slammed into him. And then something more treacherous began to swim just beneath the surface—the kind of need that hurt.

He'd only meant to grab one last thing for himself before he lost all his chances. He didn't mean to take much. He skimmed his mouth over hers, exploring. One sip, one taste. Then he thought to draw it out longer and make it into something bigger that he could take away with him. And so he took a moment to trace his tongue over her upper lip.

Then her arms snaked around his neck and he thought he felt her tremble. Before he could draw breath, she gasped against his mouth and her body was fused to his.

That changed everything.

He'd anticipated her willingness, but not the avid way she threw herself into kissing him. She was hungry and unashamed of it. Of course she was. He wanted to laugh again, but what came out of his mouth was a groan.

With the sound, she exploded in his arms, against his lips. Claiming, impelling, *daring* him to keep on.

No guile. All feeling. All his—for now. His reaction was raw instinct, the part of him without intellect rising up from the core of him and craving. He took handfuls of her hair, that glorious hair. He drank from her like a man who had been parched for a lifetime.

He wants me, she thought. The knowledge was electrifying. There was no mistaking the way his tongue swept hers, the way he held her, a little desperately. There was need there, just a little crazed. He didn't want to go away and leave her.

And she knew something else, another realization so strong and certain it was a little bit terrifying. She had never been kissed like this before.

He knew—how could he know?—that she detested insipid sweetness. That she always needed to *feel*, every hot streak of need, the surging rise of passion, the blind frenzy of wanting more, then still more. He gave that to her, on a street corner beneath a dull yellow lamp that suddenly seemed golden.

She'd known—she'd *believed*—that he was different. But until this moment, until his mouth met hers, she hadn't really understood. The place she found in his arms was one she had left behind lifetimes ago.

The heat of his mouth was familiar. There was an impatience to the way he used his tongue, something defiant in his touch that made her want to demand. Everything she needed.

He moved toward the wall without taking his mouth from hers. She went with him, stumbling a little, not willing to break their contact either. Then he pressed her against the stone, and the hard strength of his body against hers thrilled her. His mouth tried to slide to her neck, but she followed it with her own, not willing to let it go.

I want all of her, he thought. Not just her mouth, but that long column of her throat. He wanted her sweater gone so he could feel the beat of her life beneath her skin and take all that she gave. Sense was gone now, shattering into small, inconsequential pieces.

Maybe he'd just been starving for human contact. But he didn't think it was that basic. It was her...something about Shawna, and the way she shone.

"Please," she moaned against his mouth, as though she'd read his mind and was begging him into insanity. And at the sound of her voice, his blood, so heated, went to ice in his veins.

He had done many cruel things in his life. And there were several things he'd regretted. This—enjoying her, when he could offer her nothing in return—would top both lists.

How could he kiss her, start something with her, then go? He *had* to go.

Shawna felt dazed; her mouth was already swollen. She put her hands in his hair when he eased away. He caught them in his own.

"No," he said hoarsely. "Just...no. I can't."

He left her suddenly and jogged up the block. She thought of going after him again. But her knees felt like melted wax, and everything inside her was still humming, vibrating.

She'd thought he'd changed his mind. That he was going to stay. A small, keening sound left her throat. When she looked the way he had run this time, he was gone.

The man lit his cheroot by the flame of the candle on his desk, a desk that had once belonged to an earl or a count or some such dandified gentleman a cen-

tury ago. Its wood was polished to a high gloss, and
in it he could see the reflection of the flame flickering
like a snake's tongue when his warm breath touched
it.

He inhaled the smoke of the cigar and scent of the
candle. He was a man who craved sensory satisfaction
of every kind. The candle was juniper. The tobacco
was aged to perfection. The combination was sub-
lime.

He settled back in his chair and let the unhappiness
have him. "Who is she?"

The voice that came back to him over the phone
had an almost whiny edge. It was nervous. It *as-
saulted* his fine senses. "I've got no idea. She came
out of nowhere. He hasn't left that damned apartment
in six months. Now he's all over the city. With her."

"Then something has changed." The man's voice
was patient enough to be condescending. And that
made it dangerous.

But what? he thought. Cause and effect. Moving
out into the open was merely the effect. What had
caused Marsden to do so?

The woman. Something about this woman.

Marsden wasn't writing. That the man knew. It was
a simple matter these days to peer in windows, even
fourth-floor ones. There were no typewriters, no computers, no tools of the trade in Gabriel Marsden's
rented room.

So Marsden was still wallowing in the memory of
his wife, the lovely, clever and evil Julie. And he was
hiding, believing he was safe.

The man cared nothing for Marsden, as long as
Marsden did not try to write of his perceptions. Figuring out whodunit was Marsden's fame and fortune.

This change in his pattern was troubling. Until now, for six long months, the man had almost been able to forget about Marsden.

"Find out who this woman is. I want to know more about her. And let's try to avoid mistakes this time."

"Billy got carried away." That whine again. "I never told him to chase them."

"When an animal smells blood, instincts kick in." The man's fist had clenched, and the cheroot was mangled now. He disconnected.

Chasing them had been a crucial error. Marsden knew someone was aware of him now. And that changed the status quo completely.

Chapter 6

He was gone. How had Gabriel come to mean so much to her that it should matter, that he could hurt her this way in such a small space of time?

Shawna went inside, walked to the old elevator and glided upstairs to the third floor. Shawna unlocked the door and pushed, meeting with the usual resistance. Then there was the scrabbling sound of Belle's claws on the hardwood floor, and the door gave. Belle had taken to napping against the door when no one was home.

Shawna scooped the dog up in one arm. Belle wriggled and tried to lick her face. "Not now." Shawna put her down. Belle snapped at her ankle, growling.

She didn't need this now. Her blood still shivered. Her mouth still felt tender. She touched her fingers to her lips. She'd been waiting for him all her life, and he'd left her. Fate had thrown her onto his path, but he was just…stepping around her and moving on.

It wasn't supposed to be this way.

She tried to move, and Belle tripped her. The dog was darting back and forth to the door now, jumping at it, carrying on. She had to go out. Shawna sighed.

She found Belle's leash on the sideboard and bent to hook it on her collar. She realized, as she straightened, that her heart was booming hard.

Gabriel *did* want her—he'd wanted her enough to kiss her. That had to account for something. But what—toward what end—if she was never to see him again?

No. Everything inside her seemed to rise up in rebellion at the thought.

Shawna turned back to the door. The landlady's sudden equanimity aside, she tucked the Chihuahua beneath her sweater to conceal her. She stepped out into the hall, hurried for the stairs, reached the street again and set the dog down on the concrete. Belle trotted off until the leash caught her up short. Absently Shawna began to follow her.

They circled the block, and the desperate feeling in Shawna's chest built and grew. It demanded that she do something, but she wasn't sure *what*. And her time was running out.

He was leaving. Probably even tonight.

Shawna turned one more corner, heading back to the apartment. Then she saw him.

He was on the opposite side of the street, on the far corner. Waiting for her. Relief and joy bubbled up inside her. Then came the first sense of unease.

The man cut across the street and started toward her. No, not Gabriel, she thought with swamping disappointment. He was wearing the same kind of black coat, but this man did not share Gabriel's same purpose of movement. He lacked that confident, almost arrogant stride. Funny, Shawna thought, that she had managed to memorize Gabriel's walk, when mostly what she had seen him do was run. But she knew, even before the stranger drew close enough for her to make out his features, that he was not the man she wanted.

He passed beneath the street lamp. His hair was threaded heavily with silver, and the hardness about his face was cruel.

Shawna stopped and jerked Belle up short. The dog gave an annoyed yelp. They were half a block from her apartment, and if the man kept on as he was, he would intercept them before they got there. *Was* he coming toward her?

Why take the chance? *Someone* had chased them earlier.

Shawna picked up Belle. She took a single step in retreat. The man stopped as well, eyeing her, then he came toward them more quickly.

Shawna turned and ran.

She ducked into the alley behind her apartment building, Belle wriggling impatiently now, nipping at her arms so she would put her down. Shawna reached the fire escape to her apartment and she looked back sharply. She thought she saw movement in the light from the street lamps at the corner. She reached high, got one hand on the ladder, and pulled.

There was the clanging sound of metal as the ladder straightened and extended. It seemed to explode into the night, shattering the quiet. He'd hear it. But that couldn't be helped. She was fresh out of other ideas.

She climbed to the metal landing on the first floor,

then she put Belle down long enough to wrestle the ladder back into place. It came up with less clanging and clatter. She scooped Belle up again and climbed another floor.

No lights were on in any of the windows. There was no help there.

She got to the third floor, to her own apartment...and the window was locked. Oh, Katie! Of course, the window was locked. Her roommate was meticulous about security. Shawna eased back against the window, shaking.

In her lap, Belle snarled.

Down at the end of the alley, the man in the black coat finally appeared...and he paused. Shawna held her breath, her heart seeming to stop. He looked up the street, then into alley. Trying to guess which way she'd gone? Slowly, his hands in his pockets, the man started toward her. Shawna pressed herself back into the shadows, and thanked God for Katie's other eccentricity. Katie was fanatical about their electric bill. She'd turn the bedroom lights off before she'd left the apartment. The fire escape was pitch-dark.

Belle quieted.

The man reached the fire escape. Did he stop and look upward? Of course, he did. How many other places could she have gone? Except...every building on this block had fire escapes. She wondered if he would climb each and every one of them.

Then she heard his feet crunch on something littered on the concrete down there. Shawna prayed. And finally, finally, the sound of his footsteps began to recede slowly.

Shawna didn't look until the man's footsteps were so distant as to barely be heard. Then she glanced left just in time to see him turn onto the street again. She allowed herself to breath, and panic rattled in her lungs.

"Okay, Belle. Time to make hay while the sun shines." The man had turned in the direction of Third. Therefore, she could just barely get to Second before he did, and that was including if she stopped for a cup of coffee along the way.

Shawna scrambled down the fire escape. On the first-floor landing, she freed the ladder. Once again it went down with a commotion of squeaking and clanging.

She flinched, held her breath, waited. He didn't come into the alley again, and she was not going to hang around any longer to find out if he decided to return and investigate.

When her feet were planted firmly on the concrete, she realized that her knees were weak. She ran around the block unsteadily. No one was on Second, no one who looked suspicious. But how would she know?

Shawna went inside and took the steps two at a time to her apartment, afraid to wait for the elevator. She unlocked the door with hands that shook. She dumped Belle inside unceremoniously. Then she quickly locked up again behind them.

Julie Marsden's killer knew where she lived, knew where to find her.

The enormity of it hit her. Shawna scraped both hands through her hair and moved to the window. The man was not on the street now, at least not where she could see him. But he would be back. Somehow she was sure of it.

Gabriel thought he had put her safely out of this.

But someone had obviously picked up their trail again when he'd walked her home.

With that thought, the pressing weight lifted off her chest for the first time since he had left her. Shawna breathed deeply and realized she was no longer shaking.

She smiled. This changed everything.

It was just past five in the morning when Gabriel wedged his final file into the last of the cardboard boxes he'd been able to gather on such short notice. This one had come from a liquor store on the corner. It was emblazoned with the trademark of a cheap, very bad brand of whisky. He stared at the logo, and his thoughts spiraled back to Shawna.

Fine wine and three-hundred-dollar shoes.

He could have given her those things, he thought, and he would have enjoyed it tremendously. But he knew somehow that she wouldn't want them to be given. They'd only be worth anything if she'd done something to earn them.

Still, he could afford them. And here he was with a Seadog scotch box full of coroner's reports instead.

For an instant he was jarred by the contrast between the man he was now and the one he had been only six months ago. And it struck him that he had fled the comfort and luxury of his life in New York much more easily than he would be, leaving Philadelphia.

It was her, of course. Everything had been about Shawna since he'd scraped her off the sidewalk. He'd not thought seriously of his investigation since he had met her. He had done nothing constructive at all.

He settled back on his haunches in front of the box, his arms resting on his knees. For what it was worth, he thought, for what little comfort it gave, he'd seen that coming.

The memory of her had even managed to gather in this apartment despite the short time she'd spent here. Like shadows at dusk, the places where she had been were filled relentlessly and without apology with the essence of her. Over there, he thought, smiling at him, and here, cocking one brow. He had not removed her from his life any more this time than he had when he'd left the site of her mugging. It was worse this time, of course. Now—and for the rest of his days, he was somehow sure—he would remember the taste of her, the feel of her, the way she had strained eagerly against him when he'd kissed her.

He pushed her from his mind yet again and got to his feet. He looked around and tried to determine how he was going to vacate this apartment with so much to carry.

His personal possessions barely filled a duffle bag. His research filled six boxes and two paper bags. It was a problem he had not encountered before, because he'd arrived in Philadelphia with the clothes on his back. Bobby, Reynold and diligent inquiry had gradually supplied him with his files and evidence over the months. All of it had come to him via circuitous routes courtesy of the U.S. Postal Service.

It had never occurred to him that he might have to leave this place prematurely, with all of it in tow.

He sat on the vinyl sofa to work it out. Then he heard movement on the stairs.

Adrenaline was once again a sudden rage in his blood, a flood of something molten. Gabriel had one thought in his head. Answers.

He came off the sofa and crossed the room in three

fast strides. Even as he flung open the door, he knew
the risk he was taking. One bullet. One shot. That
was all it would take, and he was leaving himself
wide open, presenting himself as an easy target, one
even a five-year-old couldn't miss. He had not engaged the locks on the door when he'd come back
here this time because he knew, in some measure, that
he'd been inviting this.

Come on, come get me, who the hell are you?

But dying mattered more now than it had yesterday.

The realization and all its implications stunned him
and caused him a moment of hesitation. Now there
was a sense of wanting to come out of this alive, to
pick up the pieces, to start living again, to explore a
second chance with a dark-eyed blond who'd made
him smile.

He was over the threshold, onto the landing, even
as the door cracked back against the wall. And he had
Shawna in his hands, hands that were clenched to kill,
before he could assimilate who he had found on his
doorstep. But that moment when he'd thought of dying put him half a second behind her own reaction.

Shawna screamed and kicked him hard in the shin.

He already had her off her feet, gripping her arms
just beneath her shoulders. Gabriel gave a guttural
sound of pain and dropped her.

Shawna stumbled a little then caught herself
against the wall. "Well, hello to you, too." Her heart
was galloping.

She was back.

Pleasure swelled in his chest like warm air. It
warred with an ungodly tension that brought every
one of his nerve endings painfully and exquisitely

alive. He'd said goodbye to her. He'd closed a door in his mind. If he knew one thing, it was that he could not let her come back. Because maybe he wasn't strong enough to turn away from her a second time.

"What are you doing here?"

"I'll tell you. But first I need to sit down."

"No. Tell me here. Then go home."

She moved to look down the stairwell. "Gabriel, I'm not sure that's wise."

The way she said it, and the simple gesture, had violence rising to the surface of his blood all over again. He moved to look down, as well.

No one was there.

She wandered inside without his invitation. Gabriel turned, growled something unintelligible and followed her. This time when he shut the door, he engaged all the locks.

"Tell me," he said again. "Did someone try to hurt you?"

"No. I got away."

His heart froze.

Her eyes darted to his boxes, shadowed for a moment, then came back to his face. Her chin came up a bit, as though to ward off a blow, and her gaze, usually so direct, wouldn't quite meet his. The breath she took in was audible.

"I can't do it." She felt her skin heat, and she cursed her own heart.

She'd intended to be calm, practical, outlining all the common-sense reasons why she should stay with him. She'd meant to tell him about the man in the black coat. But her reasons for being here were so purely emotional. She couldn't let this end yet. It went against every fiber of her being.

"I can't just stand back and watch you go! That's not the way this is supposed to be. And I don't *want* to. When you left—ran again, really—I realized that. I'm just no good at giving up, especially when I really want something."

He was disbelieving. "So you thought you'd go out and get yourself killed?"

"No. I decided to walk the dog."

His head hurt.

"I'm meant to be in this with you. They've found me now. They know who I am."

His blood felt too hot, his skin too cold. "Start from the top."

She told him of spotting the man across the street, and how he had moved in her direction. How she had gotten up onto the fire escape. She finally stopped her fretful movement and hugged herself. "Someone must have been watching us when we walked from your place to mine."

He barely heard her. The truth staggered him. The killer was watching his apartment. How the hell had it happened? And how long had it been going on?

"You've taken care that no one should find you. But I was just a waitress taking the bar exam until a few hours ago. Who did I have to hide from? My phone number's listed. A million people have my address."

Gabriel didn't respond.

"Are you hearing me? By now they've got to know who I am, where I work, when I work there. Gabriel, if you run off and leave me, I've got to disappear, too. Doesn't it make more sense that we consolidate our forces and do it together?" It had taken her an hour to polish that argument. "Let me go with you. *Please.*"

He swore, one of the more colorful combinations of words she'd heard in a while.

Gabriel went to the window. She noticed that he did not stand directly in front of it as she had earlier. He kept to the side of the sofa and peered out. She had some learning to do yet if she was going to be useful.

"Did anyone follow you here?"

"No, I—"

"How can you be sure?"

"I waited until he was outside my window again— out front—then I went out the back, down the same fire escape where I hid the first time."

Gabriel left the window. "All right. Okay."

"I can come with you?"

"I'm willing to accept that you lost him."

He finally met her eyes. And in them she saw the truth. He did *not* want her here. He did not want her involved.

Shawna felt the heart drain out of her. Pride cracked. Something bled just beneath the surface. "I just thought you ought to know."

"Sit down," he said curtly. "Let me think."

A sensation of futility overwhelmed him. What in the name of God was he supposed to do with her? What was he supposed to do now? She was in danger because he'd had a bad moment and had gone downstairs in the night. Now she was his...to keep alive.

She began wandering the apartment, peering into the boxes he'd packed. "Is there food in any of these? I missed dinner."

He felt dazed. So had he, but the last thing he was feeling right now was hunger.

"There might be something in that box there under the hot plate. I was just going to leave whatever I had."

Shawna dug out a package of crackers. Gabriel winced. They had to be a week old.

She sat on the sofa and began popping them into her mouth methodically. "Gabriel," she said, swallowing. "We need some sort of plan here." She leaned forward, blond hair spilling over her shoulders. And in spite of everything, her earnest expression made him want to smile.

So he smiled. Tiredly, but he smiled.

He wanted to be able to tell her that *they* didn't have to do anything. But, of course, his chances for that had run out when he'd gone back down to the street at midnight.

"You're not getting anywhere with the evidence you've got, right?"

"Are we back to my needing a fresh pair of eyes?"

"Well, you do, but my point is that you appear to be running out of time."

How long? he wondered again. How long had the killer known where he was? A better question, he thought—why hadn't he done anything about it before this?

"Your problem is that you can't get more evidence because you're dead. But *I* can nose around and gather more information for you—the most current information. Maybe *that's* what the fates had in mind."

He stared at her. He opened his mouth to answer. Then all he could do was close it again. In that moment his adrenaline left him. Everything that had carried him through the bizarre events of the past day and night washed out of him.

She was completely and utterly out of her mind.

He went to the sofa and sat, putting his head in his hands. She was also in this—and she was in deep. And if she had any prayer at all of getting out again, she was going to have to go still deeper with him first. Gabriel dropped his hands.

"I have all the current information."

Her brows went up. "You do? How?"

"Bobby and Reynold each set up a series of information drops for me." At her baffled expression, he explained. "Computers and voice mail systems around the country. Every few days or so I call in to one of them. Bobby and Reynold leave word there about the latest goings-on. If it's an actual, physical report, they'll use post office boxes. They let me know which city, then I call in and have the mail forwarded here."

It seemed like a lifetime ago that he had last heard from Bobby, since he had learned about the DNA glitch. No, he had not put much mind to Julie's death in these last twenty-four hours.

But gut instinct had horned in. He knew that if he could figure out how that DNA matched Stern, he'd know it all. The veil would be pierced. The truth would be revealed.

He'd know who killed Julie.

Gabriel rose again and went to the window. Already, in the time that had passed since Shawna had come back, the city was waking. As he watched, a newspaper delivery truck clamored around the corner onto Second. Dawn was beginning to tint the sky a pale gray. With the city stirring, moving, the streets filling, it would be difficult to ascertain if anyone was following them.

Of course, someone would. Gabriel knew that now.

"Catch some sleep," he said suddenly. "You can have the bed."

Shawna blinked. "Sleep?"

"God only knows what's going to happen from here on in. I can't promise when you'll have another chance. So you'd better grab some shut-eye while you have the chance."

"But what about you?"

"I have to sort this out. I need time." Without the distraction of her, he thought.

He watched her do it without argument, which surprised him a little. But then he already knew she was a woman who greedily accepted her pleasures, and he supposed sleep could be counted as one of them.

He knew a mind-numbing moment when he thought she was going to peel back that blanket and curl up between his sheets, a moment when his heart slammed, and a nasty voice asked him just what he was going to do about *that*. Then she stretched her arms over her head and yawned in a fluid, catlike gesture, and she simply lay down on top of the blanket.

Shawna gave him her back because her smile had spread and she didn't want him to see it.

There was no doubt about it now. He was going to take her with him.

Chapter 7

She actually slept. From what Gabriel was able to tell, she did it deeply and dreamlessly. But he felt like a fire was burning inside him. He couldn't sit still, couldn't lie down and settle for a nap.

He allowed himself to wander a time or two into the corner of the apartment where the bed was, to watch her. Her expression was serene, her face unlined by trouble. What had he done to her?

From the first moment he saw her, he'd felt a deep need to lose himself in her light. He'd wanted to step away from the sordid and vicious memories of what had happened to Julie into the brightness that was Shawnalee Collins. And in doing so, he had risked her life.

He could not even claim he had done it unknowingly.

It rankled him—deeply—to run from this trouble. Now that he had been flushed out, a part of him wanted to stay in Philadelphia, to meet this bastard and his henchmen head-on. But if they remained here, someone would eventually come knocking at his door with weapon in hand. And as long as Shawna was with him, he couldn't risk it.

So they would leave, he thought. Together. And that complicated things immensely.

As the sun came up, he finally lay down on the sofa and dozed fitfully. But he was back at the window when Shawna awoke. She stepped up soundlessly behind him.

"I've been thinking."

Gabriel spun back to the room, his pulse instantly warring. Then, carefully, he breathed. "We're being stalked by parties unknown. Under the circumstances, it might be wise if you didn't creep up on me."

Her shoulders went back. "I didn't *creep*."

"Close enough."

"You were lost in a world of your own."

"With good reason."

She sighed. "Don't you want to know what I've been thinking about?"

"If I said no, would that stop you from sharing it with me?"

She seemed to think about it. "Probably not."

"You didn't have *time* to think," he grumbled. "You've been out like a light for the past two and a half hours." He thought maybe he was actually jealous. At this point he'd kill for that kind of sleep and her clear mind.

He turned back to the window. But he heard her moving about the apartment now, the padding of her feet on the cold, hard floor, the squeak of vinyl as she sat on the sofa. He wanted to watch her, because the way she moved, the unexpected things she did, made him want to smile.

He kept his back turned to her instead. Her life was in his hands. He would think clearly, without distractions now, if it killed him.

"It occurred to me that there's no sense in not getting a gun now," she said. "I mean, it's not like if you register for one, it will lead them to you. They already know where you are. And we really need one. We've got bad guys popping up all over the city now."

"Won't work. The waiting period for a handgun in Pennsylvania is too long. We can't risk staying here. We've got to go."

"What about New York, New Jersey, Maryland, Delaware? We're at the back door of all those places. One of them must have more lenient gun laws."

He wouldn't bet on it.

"Pick a state," she went on, "and we'll go there and you can register for a handgun. Or better yet, we could throw them a monkey wrench and I could do it."

She *was* clever. The problem, Gabriel thought, turning back to her, was that he didn't know the gun laws in Jersey or Delaware or Maryland. He knew New York's, and they were tough.

She was on her feet again. "In the meantime, I need toothpaste and a bar of soap. Shampoo would be nice, too, but I can make do without it."

He frowned. "You want to take a shower?"

"I like to be at my best when I'm running for my life."

Gabriel felt another headache coming on. "What

do I have to say to make you understand that this isn't a game?''

She looked back at him from the bathroom doorway. "You can go through life and everything it throws at you in one of two ways, Gabriel. You can be irritated by it or you can look for the bright side. Either way, everyone's days are numbered. They're going to whiz by faster than you want them to. So isn't it better to enjoy them as best you can while you've got them, no matter what's going on? What a waste, at the very end, to look back and wish you'd laughed more.'' With that, she shut the door.

It took Gabriel a moment to recover from her speech and go to his duffle bag. He dug out toothpaste and shampoo. He knocked on the door. It opened a crack, and a slender hand shot out to snag his offering. Then the door shut again and her voice came muffled from the other side.

"Thank you, Gabriel."

"You're welcome."

Gabriel went back to the window, feeling bemused.

She was in the shower for seventeen minutes. Gabriel counted every one of them.

The pipes in the old building were raucous. Over their clamor and the rush of water, he heard occasional snatches of a song. After one strident note, he went to the bathroom door, something witty on the tip of his tongue, something that sprang from the heart of the man he used to be. He raised a hand to knock, then he brought it down again slowly.

He had a sudden flash of her in there, water sluicing over her skin, running in steaming rivulets over her breasts, down those long, athletic legs, sliding over curves and angles and trailing soapy bubbles. His body's reaction was swift and strong and heated.

Every instinct he possessed backed away from it hard.

A few minutes later the door opened. Steam wafted out ahead of her, and Shawna stepped through it. His fantasy wasn't shattered, but it shifted, like the many things she made him feel from moment to moment. Her hair was slicked back wetly. Her skin was rosy. She was fully dressed again—jeans and the same lightweight sweater she'd arrived in—but the sight of her throttled him just as hard as the erotic turns his mind had just taken.

"I feel better." Her voice was light. A smile lingered about her mouth.

"Yeah. Good."

"Amazing what a little hot water can do for the spirit."

He hadn't been aware that hers had been suffering. Then again, she wouldn't let it show. If nothing else, she'd be on guard against him changing his mind and leaving her.

She was as tough as she was irrepressible. He liked this woman.

She dug into the box under the hot plate again, then she sat on the sofa with half a bag of stale chips. He watched, dumbfounded, as she examined one thoughtfully.

"You can't seriously intend to eat that."

She placed it on her tongue and closed her mouth over it, chewing. She shrugged. "You seem to be fresh out of Chateaubriand for two."

A smile flickered on his lips. "I've been doing some thinking of my own."

Her eyes narrowed. "About what?"

Hot water pouring over your skin. Gabriel cleared his throat. "They're watching this place. We've got to assume that and act accordingly."

"Okay."

"Point two—we've got to get to a telephone."

"Why?"

"I don't have one."

She let out a quick peal of laughter. This time he allowed himself to smile all the way.

"Anyway, I thought I'd check to see what gun laws our friendly neighbors are currently laboring under."

She grinned. "You listened to me."

"Of course I did."

"Sometimes, the way your face closes down, it's hard to tell."

"My face does what?"

"You get...stony."

"Stony."

She nodded, chewing the chips.

"No, I don't." That bothered him.

"No offense, Gabriel, but you can be just a wee bit...stubborn."

Oh, loosen up, Gabe. The whole world doesn't bend by your rules.

That old, lost voice came back to him without warning. Julie. Gabriel felt as though the breath had been punched out of him. For all his pursuit of the truth, the memory of her voice had gone. So had her laughter, even the slicing edge of her anger when it had so easily flared. He'd been on a mission these past six months, and he'd closed even the memories out.

But in that moment, with Shawna's comment, Julie's voice came back to him. And in his heart, Gabriel answered her. If I *had* loosened up, you'd be alive.

He pulled himself back. "I have to call around and figure out the best place to go."

Shawna watched him closely, but said nothing.

"I don't like the idea of leaving you in my apartment to do it. So we have to go together."

"I've got a telephone. We could go to my place."

"They'll be watching there, too." Gabriel paused. "But yeah, that's what I was thinking." Until they got out of this city, until they bought themselves some space and time, they'd probably be watched wherever they went. And being inside a building was a hell of a lot safer than being inside a phone booth.

"Here's how we're going to do this. We need the law on our side, but there's no way they're going to buy what's going on here, even if we tried to tell them. I could show them some kind of ID and convince them, but it would take all day and it would blow this whole thing sky-high. So we'll lie to them."

Her eyes darkened. "Oh, no."

She was too good, he thought. She was going to have to get over it.

"We'll tell them you're having a dispute with your live-in lover. He tried to hurt you. You ran. Now you need to get back into your apartment to get something, but you don't know if he's still there or not. So you're afraid to go there alone."

She saw what he was getting at. "Sort of like arranging for a police escort?"

"Exactly. They shouldn't nag you about filing a complaint since you don't have any bruises."

"There's one problem with that."

"What?"

"I *do* have a roommate. And he's a she. If Katie's there, I'm going to be hard-pressed to pass her off as my muscle-bound lover."

He laughed. The fact that he had done it—again—sobered him. "Does Katie work?"

Shawna nodded.

"Today?"

Her smile spread slowly. "The eleven-to-seven shift."

It was after ten in the morning now. By the time they got there, her roommate would be gone.

"Okay, then. I'll take my turn in the shower—" he'd considered that she had a point about hot water "—then we can get this show on the road. The cops will escort you home. You'll go inside, Lover Boy will be absent, you'll say thanks very much and show them the door. Then you'll lock up and wait for me."

Shawna frowned. "But how will you get there?"

"Trust me. When you saunter out there to meet the cops, it's going to throw our surveillance team into a tailspin. I should be able to follow you with no problem."

"They'll follow me. They'll want to know what I'm doing with the cops. And you'll follow them. With any luck, they won't think to look for you behind them." She grinned suddenly. "I like it."

She still didn't get it.

It wasn't just strategy, a game of wits, he thought. Even if she begged him to let her go now, even if she suddenly decided that she *didn't* want to accompany him, he couldn't let it happen. She was his captive. Either she didn't know it—or she didn't care.

She was supposed to take the bar exam in—

what?—a few days? Had she even realized yet that she was probably going to miss it?

Why would a woman throw away everything she had worked years for to help him, a virtual stranger? Was her faith in her higher power *that* unshakable, so strong that she would fall blindly into step with whatever it seemed to order? It was something else he would have to figure out before too long.

Gabriel turned for the bathroom. He stepped inside and shut the door behind him.

Then everything unraveled for him all over again. Hanging from the shower rod were one freshly washed pair of panties and a bra. What the hell did she have on under those clothes she was wearing?

Easy answer. Nothing.

It was going to be a very long day.

Half an hour later, Gabriel listened as Shawna rapped her knuckles against the door on the opposite side of the hallway. He stayed back, inside his own door, waiting.

Their plan depended on his neighbor's ability not to wonder why a woman would climb to the fourth floor of an apartment building to use a telephone to beg for help. It was possible he would call the cops—on Shawna. But Gabriel hadn't wanted to leave the fourth floor to do this. He had the unrealistic conviction that as long as they could easily retreat to his apartment, they were safe.

The killer hadn't bothered him here yet, after all.

From what Gabriel knew of the man across the hall, there wouldn't be a problem anyway. He'd encountered him a few times, a grizzled, elderly guy who smelled forever unwashed, with a hint of what might well have been Seadog scotch hanging over him. In fact, from what Gabriel was able to tell, Shawna had to knock three times before she roused the old gent and Gabriel heard the murmur of their voices.

When she went inside, when he heard the click of the opposite door shutting again, his muscles went as hard and fragile as glass. He'd been leaning against the inside of his door, his forearms braced against the wood. His hands curled into fists. He backed off.

Come on, come on, get it over with and come back here. As he waited, an image of one of the hundreds of photographs he'd collected flashed across his mind—Julie's throat laid open, blood running in rivulets over the concrete sidewalk.

He went to the door again. The old man was drunk half the time, for God's sake. He wouldn't wonder why Shawna needed a cop if she had a six-foot-plus pitbull by her side. Gabriel threw open the door to go over there—and Shawna stumbled inside.

"Whoa." He steadied her with a hand on each of her shoulders.

"Mission accomplished."

Gabriel took his hands back carefully. "Good."

"I have to go back downstairs now to meet the cop. I had a brainstorm and asked for the same one who investigated the day you rescued me from that mugger."

He hadn't done any such thing, Gabriel thought. She'd taken her lumps, despite his interference. But Gabriel didn't bother to say so.

He watched her move fast now, shooting her arms into the sleeves of her cardigan and going back to the door. Her jeans cupped her bottom, and he found himself staring. He roused himself from a whole new set of mental images. All these involved the skin beneath her clothing and what those little scraps of bathroom lace would look like on her.

If he kept thinking along those lines, they were both going down.

"Gabriel? Are you coming?"

"Right behind you."

By the time they reached the vestibule, Shawna's cop was there, waiting for her. There was no time to reiterate their plan. Not that they needed to, Gabriel thought. He'd forced her to go over it three or four times and it was as simple as boiling water. She'd go to her apartment, go through the motions of making sure her killer boyfriend wasn't there, and send the cop on his way. Then she'd bolt the door behind him until Gabriel arrived.

Shawna went outside onto the street, flashing a grin over her shoulder at him. Gabriel stiffened, because who the hell would she be smiling at under the circumstances? But his own mouth curled up as she slid into the back seat of the cruiser.

At least, he thought, she hadn't waved goodbye.

He waited five minutes, precisely. He figured that was as long as it would take for anyone watching to unravel themselves from their various posts and decide what to do about this strange turn of events. His best guess sent the thugs right along on Shawna's trail, but—depending upon how many of them were—they might go directly to the nearest precinct. There, they would realize that they had been duped.

Either way, Gabriel thought, they wouldn't be watching his door for a while.

He went outside and a cab turned the corner and cruised toward him the moment he stepped to the curb. Gabriel thought that maybe, just maybe, there *was* an angel watching out for them somewhere. There had been times during his stay in this city when he'd waited a full half hour for anything even vaguely resembling public transportation.

Five minutes later the cab coasted to a stop in front of Shawna's apartment building. Gabriel shoved money at the guy—probably too much, but he was getting paranoid now. He got out, looked both ways— nobody watching, nobody visible—and jogged into the lobby.

And Shawna was there.

"Damn it! You're supposed to be upstairs!"

"I got nervous. I was afraid you wouldn't make it."

There was no getting through to her. He took her elbow. "Lead the way."

"Over here."

She began moving toward an elevator. Gabriel let his hand slide down her arm until he'd caught her fingers in his, and he stopped her short. "Any stairs around here?"

"Sure, right over—" He was pulling her that way before she could finish, before she could contemplate the sensation of his hand trailing down her arm.

Upstairs she unlocked her door and pushed against it. Belle resisted with her body. There came the familiar scrabbling sound, and the door gave.

Shawna scooped up the Chihuahua. Gabriel shut and locked the door behind them. She let the dog lick her face, then she put her down again. Her cheeks were heated.

"I'm sorry."

Gabriel scowled.

"We'd have been trapped in that elevator. If they'd followed us, they could have cornered us there." She could have gotten them both killed. The realization left her shaky.

Gabriel waited a beat before answering. Ironically, while he'd wanted her to take this more seriously, watching the confidence drain out of her was painful.

"Don't."

"But I—"

"*Stop*. Stop beating up on yourself."

She stood there, watching him bleakly.

"Oh, hell," Gabriel murmured.

Don't do it, said a voice in his head. He did it, anyway. He closed his eyes and drew her into his arms. But he was rigid with control this time. And there were touches, then there were touches. He'd be okay.

Shawna felt the difference.

This gesture was meant to be one of comfort, she realized—but oh, how he'd had to consider it first. It was no more or less than what he had done when he'd opened his apartment door a short while ago and she'd stumbled inside. But that time he'd held her away from him. And this time she had a moment to look up into his face. She saw the weariness there, so deep, far older than the troubles that had come since their acquaintance.

Something rolled over inside her. He held her, and she let herself savor it again, the feeling of him against her.

She let her arms go around his waist. She tucked her face to his chest, inhaled the spice of his scent—and felt at peace again. Then a tremor went through him.

She looked up quickly. "What?"

He let her go, stepped back quickly and crossed to the window. Not because he actually wanted to see if anyone was lurking down there yet, but because he needed a moment of time.

He'd always tackled love the way he'd tackled life, he thought, finding something—someone—he wanted and going after it. If he had met this woman under different circumstances, he knew he would have gone after her hard. But he wasn't doing that. He was holding back.

Her impact on him was confusing, anyway. Constant. Every time he got near her, it was like a physical blow. He didn't know what to do with her. What to do with *this*. It came at a time when he needed to focus all his instincts on surviving.

Gabriel looked down at his hands, clenched again. It was safest, he thought, just to get back to the subject at hand.

"You're doing great," he said hoarsely. "You got us here."

Her response to that was a little snorting sound.

"Paranoia is a learned response. You'll get the hang of it." Gabriel suspected that by the end of this, she'd be as intrepid as Sherlock Holmes.

He changed gears.

"Three things. I need a phone, some paper and something to write with."

"Sure." Her voice was soft, still troubled. "I'll get it."

When she had gone down a narrow hallway, Gabriel looked around the apartment. Then he received another mild jolt.

She had told him she had a roommate. Their place

was a hodgepodge of tastes, clearly an effort at compromise between them. What startled him was how easily, how quickly, he could pick out which contributions were Shawna's.

There was an old country-style sideboard in the living room, currently in use as an entertainment center. *Hers.* There was a print in the center of one wall, ultramodern, slashes of color that were totally at odds with the simplistic taste of that one piece of furniture. But it was her, too, raw and unfettered.

His gaze skimmed further. Three bright yellow throw pillows, the color of sunshine—they had to be hers. A delicate, lacy white afghan draped casually over the back of a chair—warm comfort, hers as well. The scissor-sharp alignment of magazines on the coffee table—*not* hers. There was a stack of books on the floor. He went and scanned the titles. There were five of them, ranging from a current bestseller to a laboriously dry tome on corporate law.

It all spoke of Shawna, of the many different and complicated parts of her.

He stepped past a coffee table sitting at an odd angle, almost in the middle of the room. There he noticed the box from the mugging. He felt himself smile again.

It was still wrapped in its multitude of rubber bands. She hadn't opened it, and Gabriel found that he wasn't surprised.

He leaned over it to examine the bands, then he noticed the smell. He rubbed a hand over his nose. It reminded him of the curtains in his grandmother's house before she had died. She'd had a stroke, but independent old dame that she was, she'd refused to allow anyone to come in to clean. As a result, there'd been a dust bunny convention in that house. It had seemed to Gabriel at the time that they'd come from far and wide for the security of living in a home where a broom was never going to find them.

Yes, he thought, picking the box up, it smelled like Gram's curtains, an odd combination of sun-baked dust, old nicotine and…paper? Something he couldn't quite put a finger on.

"What are you doing?"

Gabriel turned. Shawna had come back with a pen and a legal pad. He put the box down. "Aren't you curious to know what's in here?"

She seemed to recoil. "Do you think it died? You do, don't you?"

"*Died?*"

"Something smells in there."

"It's not death." *That* he had encountered a time or two, usually along with the metallic bite of blood in the air.

"What, then?"

"I'm not sure. Let's find out."

Shawna hesitated. He realized that half of what had kept her from opening the box was uneasiness about what she would find inside. The other half was pure courtesy. The box didn't belong to her.

The dog barked. Shawna looked at the Chihuahua. "What?"

Gabriel scowled. "Dogs don't talk."

"She's trying to tell us something."

This was bordering on the ridiculous, he thought. But the mutt gave a quick, *thump-thump* with her skinny tail.

"Just toss the damned box then," he said irritably.

"But don't leave it here smelling up your living room while you're gone."

"Toss it?" Shawna repeated, horrified. "Without knowing what's inside?"

"It was given to you. It's yours now. That's my point."

Shawna hesitated, then she nodded.

She left the room again and came back with scissors and a paper bag. It took the better part of twenty minutes for them to snip away the rubber bands. Shawna kept sweeping the pile of resultant snaking strings into the bag.

Finally, Gabriel was able to lift the top off. And even he had a moment of shock.

Money. A lot of it.

"Oh, my God," Shawna breathed. *"My God."* She scooped both hands inside and came up with them brimming. Gabriel caught a twenty that drifted off the top of the pile. "She just gave this to me and walked away!"

Gabriel had recovered from his surprise. He began organizing what was still in the box, laying it out in neat denominations. Most of them were twenties.

"Where would she get it? *Where?* She didn't even have a coat!"

"Social security?" the ex-cop in him guessed. "Did she seem homeless?"

Shawna thought about it, of the faded housecoat, and how skinny Belle was. Maybe the smell of the box said it all. "She's had this stashed somewhere for a long time."

"Probably under a blanket or boxes or under leaves in the park."

"Why did she dig it out? Why did she give it to

me?'' Then Shawna sat back on her heels fast and hard. ''It all fits in.''

''What does?'' Gabriel was still counting twenties. But he glanced at her and knew in a heartbeat that he was about to hear another serendipitous explanation.

''She gave me the money. You saved me and the box. And now…Gabriel, what have you been doing for money since you died?''

''I owe Reynold a bit by now. He sends me cash every week or two. Untraceable.''

Her heart was thumping. ''Can you still use your post office box network if we're on the run? You can't, can you? We won't be able to wait anywhere long enough to have things forwarded.''

Gabriel was beginning to realize, counting the piles, that there was well over fourteen thousand dollars in the box. At the bottom there had been a nice stash of hundreds.

He looked up at Shawna. Her expression was troubled. She was struggling with the morality of it, and he felt something soft move inside him. He stopped counting.

''Shawna—''

''You don't think she robbed a bank, do you?''

''If she did, it was a while ago, and this money's been stashed all this time.'' He couldn't help it. He'd told himself he wasn't going to touch her. But he reached out to rub a thumb over the frown between her eyes. ''Did she seem like a bank robber to you?''

''No.'' Shawna sighed.

He took his hand away reluctantly. He looked at the money again. It did seem…no, he would *not* say fateful. As far as he was willing to go was…spooky. Convenient, certainly.

"We need this," he murmured.

Shawna nodded solemnly. "I know."

"I'll make you a promise. When this is over, this box will be full again. I'll see to it."

"Oh, Gabriel—"

He put a finger against her lips to silence her. And wondered where all this tenderness had come from so suddenly. He wasn't a man given to soft gestures. Had he ever been this way with Julie?

In the beginning, he thought, just maybe he'd had the inclination. But it hadn't been her style to accept such offerings. Theirs had been mostly a time of heat and of battles, of laughter and living on the edge.

The contrast disturbed him.

"It's not my money," Shawna said.

"That's why it matters that I replace it." Gabriel pulled all the piles into one and stood. It was an immense amount of cash to carry. They'd have to divide it up, he thought, which was probably safer. If one of them went down, the other would still be financially mobile. "Where's your purse?"

Her face drained of color. "You want *me* to carry it?"

"Some of it." He rolled fifteen hundred or so into two wads, and put one in each of his pockets. That still left a lot.

"Ah," she said, understanding.

When he had it divided up between them and stashed it away, he let out a breath. For whatever reason, it was all coming together. Now all they needed was a weapon.

Chapter 8

Gabriel took the legal pad and the pen into the kitchen. He used the phone there, and an hour later—an hour during which he watched Shawna pace, raid the refrigerator and peer out the window like a bad actor—he had the beginnings of a plan.

"Boo."

Shawna spun back to face the room, her eyes like saucers. She pressed a hand to her heart, barely breathing. "Don't do that!"

"Turnabout is fair play. I heard that somewhere." And he smiled.

He did it now and again, she thought, but rarely. Some grins were tight and wary, others were fleeting and tense, against his will. How priceless it was for him to really let one go, as he did now. She wanted to reach out and trace that rare, full curve of his lips.

There was so *much* feeling inside him, she thought,

and so much rigid control containing it. She wondered if even he knew how hard he fought his emotions.

She did not think he would run again if she touched him now. He seemed to have taken responsibility for her. But, for reasons she didn't entirely understand yet, Shawna kept her hands to herself. She pushed them into her jeans pockets.

"Good news?" She raised her brows, crossing to him.

"More like the absence of bad. Maryland and Delaware are out. New York and New Jersey have possibilities."

Shawna leaned her elbows on the breakfast bar. She reached and turned the legal pad around so she could read his scribbling. His handwriting was atrocious.

"It's a matter of who you know there and how much they like you," he explained.

Shawna frowned. "Do you know anyone in New Jersey?"

"No. But I do in New York."

It would have to be Reynold, he thought. Bobby might have minimal clout within the NYPD, but he wouldn't be able to manage what Gabriel was about to ask. For this he needed a politician. Gabriel called the *Monitor*.

He asked for the editor and was given the usual hemming and hawing. "Tell him Gabriel Marsden is alive." What the hell, Gabriel thought. In for a penny, in for a pound.

There was a long pause before another extension picked up. This line was filled with some surface static and the normal chaos of a large daily newsroom in the background. "Who is this?" came another voice.

"I need to speak with Reynold Austin. Tell him it's Gabe Marsden and see if he picks up the line."

The voice put him on hold again. Reynold didn't pick up the line. Instead, Gabriel got the man's secretary. He went through the same routine.

Finally, Reynold's voice boomed into the phone. "What the hell is this about?"

"I need your help, Reynold."

Stone silence, Gabriel thought, and he almost smiled again. He wondered how Reynold's heart was these days.

Then Shawna came closer, inching around to his side of the breakfast bar as though to pick up some of the other man's conversation. The warmth of her, that sunflower scent, enveloped him. Gabriel held up one finger to warn her off, but it did no good. She didn't move, and for a moment his mind went blank.

"*Gabe?*" Reynold said, breaking the spell.

"He found me, Reynold."

"But *how? How* did it happen?"

A very good question, Gabriel thought. "No one's leaned on you?"

"Nobody's spoken your name to me in months now."

Gabriel thought about that. It might be true. It might not be. *Someone* had let it out that he was alive. And only Reynold and Bobby knew.

It was an ugly, painful realization that had been nagging him for hours now. If Julie's killer had traced him to Philadelphia, then he almost had to have done it through the telephone setup, or the post office box link. The killer would have to have found one of them and traced the trail back.

Reynold or Bobby. Bobby or Reynold. It hurt. Hell, it did.

"I need a gun," Gabriel said levelly, clearing his mind again.

There was a space of quiet. "I could have one shipped to you, unregistered."

"No." Gabriel was even less willing now than he had been days ago to be picked up with an unregistered weapon. If his backside got thrown in jail now, Shawna was on her own. "I want to do this on the up-and-up."

"Under your own ID?"

"No. I'm going to give you a name." His heart clenched. His blood slowed. Was he killing her?

Shawna shrugged easily and without qualm, then she nodded. Gabriel put his hand over the phone. "It'll leave a trail leading straight to you."

"They already know who I am."

He rubbed a hand over his forehead. "You shouldn't trust me like this."

"I have to."

It was so simple for her, he thought. "If you have any kind of record, now's the time to come clean with me."

"Who, me?"

Stupid question, he thought. "Okay. Never mind." He turned his attention back to the phone. "The name's Shawnalee Collins." He gave various other necessary information, then he paused. "Can you help?"

"Probably. I guess you're not going to give me a number where I can reach you."

"Same thing goes, Reynold. It's safer all the way around if I don't. And we're going to have to leave the voice mail alone from here on in."

There was a pause while Reynold digested this. "You don't think—"

"I don't know how it happened. But they were my only risk."

"Gabe." Another pause. "You're sure you know what you're doing?"

He looked at Shawna again, at those hopeful brown eyes, at her half smile as she waited for some good word. "Absolutely not."

Reynold chuckled, but it was a strained sound. "I'll see what I can manage. Don't try to buy anything until I pave the way first."

"Thanks. I'll call you later tonight. At home." Gabriel hung up the phone.

"Well?" Shawna asked expectantly.

He looked at her and let the last of his sanity slip away. "Been to New York lately?"

Shawna watched out the window as the cab Gabriel had called pulled up outside. The driver got out and looked up at the building when he found no one waiting for him. Shawna opened the window and leaned out to wave.

Gabriel dragged her inside again by the back of her T-shirt. He tried not to think about the lack of a bra strap underneath. He tried even harder not to think of what could have happened in that split second while she'd been a wide-open target.

She gaped at him. "You can't honestly think someone's going to pick me off while I'm hanging out my window." Every once in a while, she managed to forget what was going on—her mind skipped around the *reason* they were together. Now her nerves felt like rubber bands stretched to their limit again.

"Let's go," he said.

Shawna started to follow him to the door. Then she stopped at the breakfast bar. "Wait. I have to leave a note for Katie."

"No." His voice was like a gunshot.

She looked up at him. "I have to."

"No. You don't. If nothing else, you could be putting her in danger."

The color drained from her face. Gabriel scrubbed his hands over his own, wishing he could grab the words back. "They won't hurt her."

"You don't know that."

But he did. It was just another gut instinct—along the lines of being sure that if he could figure out the DNA glitch, he'd have the whole picture—but it felt right. "He's known where I am for a while now, I think. No one moved on me until—" Until she came along.

Then his patterns had changed. He was doing things now, behaving in a way that the killer didn't understand. And maybe that meant Gabriel could be considered a threat again.

Gabriel began pacing. "This is no cutthroat, crazed serial killer."

Shawna's breath rattled a little as she let out a sigh. "Glad to hear it."

"He's *thinking*. He's not irrational. He's got Julie and Talia's blood on his hands, but he doesn't want more unless it's absolutely unavoidable, unless he needs to kill to keep himself off death row." The worst-case scenario—and Gabriel would *not* say this aloud—was that the killer might have his henchmen lean on Katie to get her to tell what she knew.

The problem, of course, was that the woman would know nothing. She had nothing to reveal. Would the killer believe that?

"I changed my mind. Leave a note. Tell her you've just taken off for a while. Don't tell her the truth."

Shawna's eyes narrowed, heated. "So if anyone comes around asking about me, she can show it to them. It's like using her."

"It's like protecting her."

She swallowed with exquisite care. "Right. But I've got to tell her something. I'll say I've gone back to Kansas to visit my family. Then she'll tell the diner to pull me off the schedule, and that will take care of my job, as well. Two birds with one stone."

"Why would you suddenly run off to—where did you say?—Kansas, a few days before you take the bar exam?"

"I'll tell her I decided not to take it."

He saw in her eyes that she meant it.

Ah, he thought. This was a whole new kettle of fish, and it explained part of what troubled him—why she would do this for him, why she would shelve her entire life to run away by his side. But maybe she wasn't shelving something she wanted all that badly.

A law degree? After all the years of schooling it had required? More complexity, he thought, more layers. Probably more oddball integrity. She would have some kind of reasoning that would be crazily sensible, utterly her.

But the discussion would have to wait for another time.

"She won't call your family?"

Katie might, Shawna thought. It sort of depended upon how long they'd be gone, and she knew it was senseless to ask him that. How long did it take to unmask a killer who was determined to remove your interference?

Her skin pulled briefly into gooseflesh. Shawna fought the sensation off and picked up the pencil again, writing quickly.

"I'll ask her not to try to reach me for a while because I need time to think without everyone telling me what I should do." She paused, looking up again, her eyes haunted. "Are you sure she's not in any danger?"

He'd never actually said that, Gabriel thought. "I doubt it. I really doubt it."

If the killer's men approached Katie, they'd be civilized. He *had* to go with his gut on that. The goons would ask where Shawna had gone. And Katie would repeat what she'd been told. Better yet, she would volunteer the note. They'd know, instantly, that Shawna had lied to her.

Gabriel picked up the two small bags she'd packed. "Come on." But she began wandering around the apartment, slowly and deliberately. "*Now* what are you doing?"

"Saying goodbye."

He had no time for her words to process through his brain before his body reacted to them. An unseen horse kicked him in the chest. "Shawna. Don't. You'll be back."

"Maybe not for a while."

No, Gabriel thought, probably not for a while.

At the door he stepped aside, figuring that under the circumstances, she would take care of the business of opening it and locking it again behind them. But when she stepped up beside him, she was cradling the ugly little dog in her arms.

"We don't have time for you to say goodbye to everything—"

She cut him off with a surprised cry. "I'm not saying goodbye to her. We're taking her with us."

This time he felt like his blood drained out of him. And with it went the best of his control. "Put the damned dog *down.*"

Shawna took a step back at his tone. "I can't do that."

"You can't *do* it?" He was shouting. She flinched a little. "*You can't do it?* Lady, we are running for our *lives* here! We're going to New York to get a *gun!* And you want to take pooch along?"

"Her name is Belle."

"I don't give a damn if her name is hallelujah!"

"Don't be sarcastic, Gabriel." She watched him breathe. Deeply. Evenly.

"Why, precisely, would you think it's a good idea to take a dog with us?"

"Because we want to come back alive." His complexion darkened. Shawna rushed on. "She's part of all this. Think about how I got her."

"Some guy punched you."

"No, no, before that. He punched me because that old lady stopped me and gave me that box and this dog. If she hadn't done that, I wouldn't have met you. And we wouldn't be standing here now. Nor would we have the cash to keep going. Gabriel, it's all part of a plan. *Think* about it. Not a single bad thing has happened to me since that woman pushed Belle on me. Why rock the boat?"

He couldn't believe this. "We ran through half of Philly with a thug on our tails!"

"We lost him."

"Some guy chased you up a fire escape!"

"He didn't climb it, did he?"

The dog was still wriggling in her arms. Gabriel looked at it again and knew in that moment that he was not going to win this argument. Had he *ever* won one, since the moment she'd come into his life?

She was going to make one hell of a lawyer.

He thought that he could stand here trying to get her to leave the beast behind—in which case they might get on the road sometime around noon tomorrow. Or he could acquiesce, and they could be on their way. In either scenario, pooch was probably going to be their traveling companion.

"There's one other thing," she said.

"What?"

"It's not just that taking Belle with us would be good luck. It's more like if I left her behind, it would be very *bad*. Katie doesn't particularly like her."

"Smart woman." The dog chose that moment to look at Gabriel and growl.

"If I leave Belle here, Katie will grab the opportunity to whisk her off to the pound. But that woman wanted me to have her, Gabriel. Her and the money. And we're using the money, so I have to take care of the dog. It's the principle of the thing."

Gabriel turned for the door again.

"Okay?" she said, her voice hitching somewhere between hope and wariness.

He couldn't believe he was agreeing to this. "Bring the dog."

"Thank you, Gabriel."

The mutt yipped once, quickly. "Shut up," he said. Shawna smiled.

"She called the cops," the caller said.

There were no candles this time as the man listened to the edgy voice when it reported in. The sun—that blinding, cruel sun he so hated now—was creeping in through a crack between the drapes, trying to steal into his office.

It had seemed so simple from the start, a matter of being careful, lying low, until John Thomas Stern died for his crimes. But now...now here was this woman.

Things had not gone totally awry. He'd learned her name now, through contacts with the police. She was Shawnalee Collins.

Mere days ago she had had no connection to Gabriel Marsden or John Thomas Stern. He didn't know where she had come from. But now she had called the police, apparently to avoid talking to the caller's men. It was clever move. She intrigued him.

"Where is she now?" he asked.

"Inside her apartment."

"Alone?"

"Marsden's with her."

The man didn't answer.

"You want me to try to get to her again?"

The man thought about it. "Not yet." He'd decided he wanted her. But he'd prefer to wait until she was alone to take her.

There was no telling what Marsden might do if she was snatched out from under his nose. This was assuming that the imbeciles could even arrange it. It was possible that Marsden could prevent them from getting to her. And then, of course, she would be even more careful from here on in, making it more difficult.

The caller's ineptitude was galling, but the man wasn't in a position to buy the best at this point. His money could not save him now. Leverage could.

He wanted this woman. It would be well worth the risk to talk to her himself, he thought. To have her brought here so *he* could question her about what she knew, and how exactly she'd gotten involved. Of course, if he was going to remain safe, he would have to get rid of her afterward.

"Watch her. Keep close to her," he said. "And wait until she's alone. Then take her."

"Whatever you want."

"Bring her to me."

His heart accelerated with the first pure anticipation he'd felt in months now. Marsden had always had exquisite taste in women.

It was a pity so many of them had to die.

Chapter 9

They took the cab to Gabriel's apartment, where they collected his files. They went as far as Allentown, then sent the cab with the files on to a place in upstate New York called Kiryas Joel and rented a car.

They exchanged the car for a cab in New Jersey. Now they were heading north again with Belle curled on the seat between them. There was food. They'd stocked up on munchies at a store across the street from the car rental place. Shawna had honey-roasted cashews and some caraway-studded bagel chips.

She was starting to get into the sheer challenge of besting the man who had taken Julie's life. But Gabriel was not enjoying the adventure.

He sat by the other door, staring out through the glass. Every once in a while his fists clenched, then he deliberately relaxed them again. Tight lines bracketed his mouth.

She wanted to go to him. To slide over the seat

and soothe those lines away with her fingertips, to ease the fear and the worry away. It hurt to know that in some measure, her involvement had caused it. But she kept her hands to herself.

Sometime during the ride she'd figured out that she was afraid to touch him again.

Falling for him would be like riding a trapeze without the safety net. She had never cared a fig for *safe*. She'd always taken chances. She believed in experiencing everything life handed out. In embracing it, good or bad. But maybe she had never loved before.

Was that what this was? For all of his grim moods and his serious pursuit of this killer, maybe *because* of those things, he was edging his way in on something fundamental deep inside her. Her stomach rolled over briefly, queasily. She'd only known him for two days. Did that matter? Probably not. Not everything in this world followed the rules that man, with his self-inflated logic, laid down. Some things were simply illogical, and no less true for that.

She cared deeply about Gabriel's quest—but part of that, she admitted, had certain selfish overtones. His fear touched her, because he was so strong. His sorrow hurt her, because he did not give his heart freely. And his honor, integrity and perseverance gave her comfort, because somewhere along the line she had stopped believing in them. She continued to demand them of herself, but she no longer expected them from others.

Yes, she thought, she cared. More than was sane. Because even as she fell deeper and deeper into this, into *him,* she could not forget that he didn't want her here. He'd prefer to be running on his own.

"Gabriel, I know this is dangerous. I'm not crazy."

He looked away from the window to glance at the dog on the seat between them. "No. You have no idea."

"I was *on* that fire escape."

He thought about that, nodded and waited for her to finish. That was so like him, she thought. Holding to doing the right thing, whether it appealed to him or not.

"It's just that...this is meaningful." She couldn't explain without telling him about the bar exam. She took a breath. "I've spent the past five years in law school. You know, I thought I'd end up in a courtroom someday, struggling to save the world."

"Then you'd come home, kick off your expensive shoes and drink good wine." He finally smiled. "So what happened?"

"Law isn't what I thought it was."

"You had images of Perry Mason."

Shawna nodded. She was unashamed of that.

"Truth, justice and the preservation of the American way."

"Not large tobacco settlements because somebody never did get around to quitting smoking. Not six and a half million for getting hit by a bus because you weren't paying attention, so now it's the other guy's fault and he has to pay. Gabriel, that's not *law*. At least, it's not the intent of it as our forefathers saw it."

"You're an idealist."

"Yes." There was no sense in denying that, either. "But maybe I was confusing law with *justice*. There may be very little good left in lawyering, but justice remains true. It's just sometimes neglected, forgotten, in the pursuit of other things, like the almighty dollar.''

"And this is justice? Staying with me, risking your life?''

"An opportunity to be part of something like this doesn't come along every day. It's a chance to make a difference.''

Gabriel didn't know whether to laugh or to cry.

It had bothered him—considerably—that she would do this without looking back. Because sane people did not throw their entire lives away to help a stranger. Now he understood a little better.

"Our laws say it's a crime to kill someone,'' she went on. "It's the most heinous wrong man can commit. So it's meaningful to find out who did this to Julie and Talia. To see him punished for it. Because once again, the system is letting us down. It would be unforgivable to know something's wrong with that trial—that Stern is actually innocent and someone else is guilty—and do nothing about it, to…to let the wheels of justice grind on, taking this whole issue off in the wrong direction, to let the system convict the wrong man.''

"Maybe Stern did it.'' Gabriel felt compelled to point that out. Maybe she was throwing herself into something that wasn't virtuous at all. "Maybe I'm nuts.''

"You know you're not.''

Her sentiment wasn't blind, he thought. He'd told her what he knew—the crux of the whole thing, although she hadn't yet seen his files. And she believed Stern was innocent.

"I'm glad to be a part of this, Gabriel.''

"A pursuit of justice.''

"Yes."

He felt some of the tension ease out of his shoulders again. Oddly, her skewed viewpoints sometimes had a way of putting things into perspective.

He took her hand and held it, looking down at their clasped fingers, knowing that he ought to regret touching her. She was only here, risking her life, because a faceless man had left them no choice, because he would make Gabriel pay for the crime of wishing, for one midnight hour, that he could have her.

But for a moment, being close to her restored some of his soul.

It was nearly nine o'clock when they closed in on New York city. They worked their way across the city on Forty-second Street, moving reasonably smoothly in the late traffic. The cab delivered them to the Hyatt.

Gabriel had considered—briefly—going back to his own apartment. He'd thought of hiding in plain sight. It was more of a gamble than he wanted to take with Shawna's life. So they would lie low in Reynold's territory, but they'd do it with a modicum of comfort.

He could give her that much.

Shawna got out of the cab. The hotel's lights sparkled over her like diamond raindrops. She threw up one hand—Belle was still cradled in the other—and laughed aloud.

"Come on," he said tersely, "let's see if we can get a room."

They could. It was a weekday in April, and one was available.

He had a bad moment as he finished filling out the registration form when he glanced to his side and Shawna was gone.

Gabriel jerked around, his heart accelerating until he found her wandering through the mirrored elevator bay. He let the bellman take their bags—her two large ones and his pitiful one—and went to join her.

Gabriel waited for someone from security to come and ban the Chihuahua. No one bothered. Gabriel imagined that they had seen odder things.

"How long before we have to call Reynold?" she asked.

"We'll give it another hour or two."

Shawna nodded. "I'm hungry again."

"You've got to be kidding. You've been chewing for the past six hours."

She cocked a brow at him. "That was just munchies. Let's get something to eat."

His nerves were beginning to sing, being out in the open like this. Maybe he had proven to be smarter than the killer's henchmen—at least for a while. But it seemed *too* quiet. Like the calm before the storm. Where *were* those guys? They'd chased them from the coffee shop, had chased her up the fire escape, and now…nothing.

His convoluted path to New York hadn't been that tough to unsnarl.

"Humor me?"

"Sure."

That easily, he thought. "Let's eat in the room." It was senseless to take chances when they didn't have to.

He chose an elevator and they bulleted upward. Seconds later—seconds during which Shawna felt as though she'd left her stomach back on the lobby floor—they stepped out into more mirrors. She was literally starting to feel dizzy.

They found Room 4303 and stepped inside. Her pulse felt as if it was dancing.

It was a suite, with a wet bar, a sofa, and a wide-screen TV. Beyond the sitting area was—she guessed—a bedroom, through one partially closed door. The room had a feeling of coziness and intimacy about it, even as it was elegant.

Shawna put the dog down and hugged herself. She turned about to face Gabriel.

They'd been together through the better part of forty-eight hours now. But they'd been running, moving, planning. Now all they could do was wait. In seductive comfort. But she already knew that Gabriel wasn't a man to give in to seduction easily.

She watched him shrug out of his coat and drop it over the sofa without looking at her. Being careful *not* to look at her, she thought.

She'd never had a man run from her—literally *run*—as many times as he had. When he touched her, when he so rarely touched her, it was something he recoiled from.

In the beginning she had understood. He'd been steering clear of her, holding her at arm's length, because not to do so would mean embroiling her in something dangerous. But now she was embroiled. She was in. She was running with him. And *still* he resisted her.

"There have to be room service menus around here somewhere," he muttered.

Shawna stiffened. Her stomach was suddenly full with a rocky sensation that precluded hunger after all.

"Television?" He turned to the coffee table and found the remote. "They have in-room movies. Not the video variety, but first run."

Who cared?

He turned the television on and scanned the channels. He finally found a movie. "Well," he said, and deposited the remote back on the table.

In all her life, she had never been one to hedge her bets or pussyfoot around a problem. Tackle them head-on and fix them, she thought. He wasn't immune to her. He'd kissed her. Something ached inside her as she remembered the way she'd felt in his arms.

He'd kissed her, then he'd withdrawn again. Oh, yes, she thought, it was crazy to let herself care, to let herself want him.

"What is it?" she said aloud. And she found she didn't have to explain her question.

He turned away from the television. The blue of his eyes had gone to slate. "I can't give you anything." And what scared him in a place so deep he hadn't known he possessed it was the new, sudden urge to add, *not yet.*

He couldn't speak those words. How unfair it would be to start something with her that he couldn't finish, because a killer—and whoever was in charge of the fate she so steadfastly believed in—was busy taking away all of his chances.

So forget it. Run now. You've got fourteen thousand dollars. Start living again. Let all this blow over. Go somewhere where the killer can't find you.

The voice of longing was serpentine in his head. But he could not abandon Julie.

He would do for her in death what he had not done in life. He would stand with her. He would stand for her now, when she could not do it for herself.

He would finish this.

Shawna watched him. She still hugged herself, and

her eyes were darker than brown. Lilac shadows were beginning to gather beneath them. It had been a rough two days.

He couldn't give her what she was asking for—the intimacy she wanted from him—and the sheer willpower that kept him from it made him hurt. But there *was* something he could give her, he thought, something good, perhaps, that she could take away from all this.

"Sit down."

"What?"

"Just sit."

She moved uncertainly to the sofa and sank down onto the cushions, frowning.

Gabriel went to the courtesy bar. They wouldn't have what he needed. He found the key and went through the cabinet anyway.

Nothing. He unlocked the refrigerator.

And there it was, lying neatly on its side. What, he wondered, were the odds of finding an '89 Latour in a courtesy bar?

He discovered glasses and poured one. He took her the wine. When she reached for it a little bemusedly, he held it away. "Welcome to the penthouse floor."

She scowled. "I don't understand what you're up to."

Was that wariness in her eyes now? So, he thought, he *could* make her nervous. He placed the wine on the coffee table and knelt in front of her. "Give me your feet."

"What?"

"You heard me."

"Have you taken leave of your senses?"

Probably, Gabriel thought. But it had happened two days ago.

He caught her ankle. No three-hundred-dollar heels, he thought. There was only so much he could do on short notice. He unlaced one sneaker, then the other.

He didn't put them aside. He tossed them over his shoulder.

And she understood. Shawna laughed, a clear, ringing sound, throwing her head back and letting it take her. But her eyes felt hot, as though some part of her wanted to cry. This capacity for tenderness—that it was there, and that it had survived the tension and chaos of what had happened to his life—could be her undoing.

He stood again and pulled her to her feet. "Over here."

He took the wine in one hand, hers in the other. He led her to the window. He let go of her hand and opened the blinds, then he stood behind her so she'd get the full view.

Shawna let her breath out. City lights. Another high-rise rose to her right, glittering. Skyscrapers burned on the skyline. And someone had thrown a handful of gold and diamonds beyond them, as far as the eye could see.

Her throat closed suddenly and hard. He never gave her what she expected.

He handed her the wineglass, reaching around her to place it in her hands. After a moment he let himself hold her. Lightly, his arms around her waist. Just for a moment.

"It's not the same as earning it. But it's what I can give you."

Shawna turned to him. She reached a hand up this time without thinking about it. Without *letting* herself think about it. She was going with her heart, and her fear could be damned. She touched his cheek and wondered how she could tell him that this was the part of him she needed most.

This time he didn't back off. Hope stirred in her heart.

Then the phone rang.

Chapter 10

The quiet of the room came jangling apart. Shawna cried out and nearly dropped her wine. Gabriel pivoted sharply to look at the telephone on the end of the bar.

It trilled again. Three rings, four. They both stared at it.

"Wrong number?" Shawna said hopefully.

"Possibly." Not likely.

Gabriel went to the bar. He picked up the phone and barked a hello. He listened for a moment and when he spoke his words were clipped enough that he almost spat them. "I'll be there, then."

Shawn inched closer to the bar as he hung up. "What?"

"That was easy. We've got ourselves a gun."

But Shawna's heart was skidding. "*We* were supposed to call *Reynold*." She was sure that was the way they had left it.

Play TIC-TAC-TOE and get FREE GIFTS

HOW TO PLAY:

1. Play the tic-tac-toe scratch-off game at the right for your FREE BOOKS and FREE GIFT!

2. Send back this card and you'll receive TWO brand-new Silhouette Intimate Moments® novels. These books have a cover price of $4.25 each in the U.S. and $4.75 each in Canada, but they are yours to keep absolutely free.

3. There's no catch. You're under no obligation to buy anything. We charge nothing — ZERO — for your first shipment. And you don' have to make any minimum number of purchases — not even one

4. The fact is, thousands of readers enjoy receiving books by mail from the Silhouette Reader Service™ months before they're available in stores. They like the convenience of home delivery, and they love our discount prices!

5. We hope that after receiving your free books you'll want to remain a subscriber. But the choice is yours — to continue or cancel, any time at all! So why not take us up on our invitation, with no risk of any kind. You'll be glad you did!

YOURS FREE
A FABULOUS MYSTERY GIFT!

We can't tell you what it is... but we're sure you'll like it!

A FREE GIFT—
just for playing
TIC-TAC-TOE!

DETACH AND MAIL CARD TODAY!

With a coin, scratch the gold boxes on the tic-tac-toe board. Then remove the "X" sticker from the front and affix it so that you get three X's in a row. This means you can get **TWO FREE** Silhouette Intimate Moments® novels and a **FREE MYSTERY GIFT!**

PLAY TIC-TAC-TOE

YES! Please send me the 2 Free books and gift for which I qualify. I understand that I am under no obligation to purchase any books, as explained on the back of this card.

345 SDL CX7W

245 SDL CX7Q
(S-IM-12/99)

Name:		
	(PLEASE PRINT CLEARLY)	
Address:		Apt.#:
City:	State/Prov.:	Zip/Postal Code:

Offer limited to one per household and not valid to current Silhouette Intimate Moments® subscribers. All orders subject to approval.

PRINTED IN U.S.A

The Silhouette Reader Service™ — Here's how it works:

Accepting your 2 free books and gift places you under no obligation to buy anything. You may keep the books and gift and return the shipping statement marked "cancel." If you do not cancel, about a month later we'll send you 6 additional novels and bill you just $3.57 each in the U.S., or $3.96 each in Canada, plus 25¢ delivery per book and applicable taxes if any.* That's the complete price and — compared to the cover price of $4.25 in the U.S. and $4.75 in Canada — it's quite a bargain! You may cancel at any time, but if you choose to continue, every month we'll send you 6 more books, which you may either purchase at the discount price or return to us and cancel your subscription.

*Terms and prices subject to change without notice. Sales tax applicable in N.Y. Canadian residents will be charged applicable provincial taxes and GST.

If offer card is missing write to: Silhouette Reader Service, 3010 Walden Ave., P.O. Box 1867, Buffalo, NY 14240-1867

BUSINESS REPLY MAIL
FIRST-CLASS MAIL   PERMIT NO. 717   BUFFALO, NY

POSTAGE WILL BE PAID BY ADDRESSEE

SILHOUETTE READER SERVICE
3010 WALDEN AVE
PO BOX 1867
BUFFALO NY 14240-9952

NO POSTAGE
NECESSARY
IF MAILED
IN THE
UNITED STATES

"Maybe Reynold is being extraordinarily accommodating. That was the owner of a place call Apollo Weaponry out in Brooklyn. We can stop in and handle the transaction at our convenience. They open at eight-thirty in the morning."

Her blood drained. "It's a setup."

Gabriel was cold inside with the same thought.

Reynold—honorable, stand-by-his-side Reynold—would not have a third party contact him. It was too risky. And he hadn't even told Reynold where they were going to be.

So how had Reynold known? And who the hell had he contacted?

The last thing Gabriel had said to him was I'll call you tonight. At home. Maybe with the way things had blown so off course lately his memory was off. But Shawna remembered the same thing. I'll call you tonight. At home.

"Ah, damn it." He couldn't even work up anger.

"Gabriel..."

He pushed her hand away when she reached for him this time. She pulled back, her face going pale. But then, she'd been pale for hours now anyway, he thought. She was pushing herself to the wall. For him.

"I'm sorry." The words choked him.

"No. I am."

"Stop it!"

He saw her slight flinch, and he felt like hell. Ah, damn it, he thought again, but he could not find another apology. He could barely explain why he was snapping at her.

"Stop being so...understanding. I can't take it right now. The world's a vicious, rotten place, and it just bit me. Don't try to whitewash it."

If he took away the compassion he wanted to give then she didn't know how to reach him.

She swallowed what she had been about to say, the comfort she wanted to give him. But she needed to ease this for him. He wouldn't take what it was her natural inclination to give, so she would be practical instead.

"We have to go now, Gabriel. Right away."

"Yeah."

She watched him, saw his misery, and for a brief moment she hated. It was nearly an alien emotion to her, but it was sizzling, strong. Damn you, Reynold, damn you for hurting him! And, she thought, for pulling no punches. The man hadn't even tried to be coy about it! The phone call was like a slap in the face, a gauntlet thrown down.

Something about that bothered her, but there was no time to think about it now. Anyway, there was no denying that the phone call had happened.

She left him and went in search of Belle. She found her in the bedroom, ensconced like a miniature queen on the pillows of the king-size bed. "Sorry, little one," she murmured, picking her up. "Looks like it's time to boogie."

But when she went back to the sitting area, Gabriel was still standing by the bar.

"Someone knows we're here," she said, and she let a little of her anger out. "And damn it, they think we're stupid! Did you tell them we'd pick up the gun?"

Now his eyes narrowed as they moved to her. "Yeah. I played it out."

Of course he had. "When?"

"First thing in the morning."

"Then someone's probably going to come for us tonight. And I, for one, am not going to be here when it happens."

He finally moved.

Their bags were still near the door, where the bellman had left them. Gabriel hefted one in each hand. Shawna carried the dog and picked up the other.

It was a pity, she thought, that they weren't going to enjoy this room.

She thought about the wine, the shoes, what he had done, and her heart hurt with thoughts of where that might have gone. But the memory made her realize that he had tossed her sneakers God-knew-where. She was stepping out into the hallway in socks. She went back and found them and put them on while they waited for the elevator.

"Now where?"

"I'm not sure."

They stepped into the elevator. So much effort, she thought, in arranging for that gun. All for naught. And there was an added insult—she'd never even gotten dinner.

The elevator dropped like a stone thrown off a mountain peak. Once again it took her stomach a moment or two to catch up. They stepped off the car into the lobby again with no true idea of what they should do next. She glanced at Gabriel, hoping he felt less terrified and overwhelmed than she did.

His face was closed again, his eyes wary and cold. Her heart broke for him.

"They'll be there by eight-thirty. Count on it."

The voice was nearly more offensive with good news than it was when it whined, the man thought.

The caller was, of course, expecting a pat on the back. A nod of praise that would allow him to breathe more easily for a little while. The man would not give it.

He could not afford to.

He did, however, approve of the caller's initiative in going into Shawnalee's apartment once she and Marsden had gone.

The man swiveled in his desk chair, in leather that was soft as butter, smooth as a woman's skin. He reached for the fax again.

It was grainy. Shadowed. And far, far too small. The caller had warned that it was five years old. It was a photo from her college year book.

Shawnalee Collins.

The man's breath shortened until he deliberately caught it and steadied it again. He would not say that she was beautiful, but he did not care for beautiful woman. Like Julie's, her face was too unique to fall into that mold. Julie had been stunning, all angles, sharp lines. This woman possessed the aura of Eve— of the earth, born for man.

She had eyes that just hinted of laughter. An odd smile, not quite full, as though she knew a secret. She was the best of both worlds, he thought greedily—a dark-eyed blond.

She'd fascinated him from the start, from the time she had first popped up in the middle of this. Now he was beginning to crave her.

He would like very much to touch her, he decided. If everything worked well, that might happen soon now.

Apollo's was a public place. The caller assured him that it was on a stretch of four-lane highway, with an abandoned warehouse beside it. Even imbeciles such as he had working for him should be able to draw her off, away from Marsden, for a moment.

Perhaps, he thought, as early as this new day, he would meet her.

"Bring her directly here when you get her," he said.

"What about Marsden?"

But the man was no longer concerned with Gabriel Marsden at all.

He stroked a finger over the faxed photograph. She'd played games with him, of course—that note she'd left for her roommate was silly. But she was not a silly woman, so she would have known that.

It was her message to him, the man was sure. She had saved him unnecessary steps. Thanks to Shawnalee's foresight, it had not been necessary to waste precious time pressuring the roommate to find out where Shawnalee had gone.

Technology had taken care of that for him.

The caller had checked her telephone for the last number dialed. The *New York Monitor*. Reynold Austin, of course. And Austin's phone lines had been tapped for months.

Manhattan had been a shot in the dark. But Marsden would want to wait somewhere close by Austin, to minimize time when arrangements for the gun came through, and he would want to do it in his old, usual style. That narrowed it down even more. Marsden was predictable, the man thought sadly. And that was a bore.

But Shawnalee, he thought. Ah, Shawnalee. She was a different story.

Now she was safely tucked away in a forty-third-floor room, waiting for morning and the gun the man suspected she already knew she would not buy. She seemed keenly intelligent, the man thought with a swell of appreciation and anticipation. She would have figured that out by now. She knew she was coming to him. She was biding her time.

The man's chest tightened briefly. In the meantime she was alone there with Marsden. For a moment he hated Marsden again, with all the passion and all the fury he had ever experienced for the man.

Don't touch her. She's mine.

But of course Marsden would try. He always tried.

"You there?" the caller asked when the silence drew out.

"Bring her to me," the man said. "Get her away from him now as soon as possible. Take whatever chances you have to."

He was getting tired of waiting. And really, he had never been a patient man.

It seemed that the night would never end.

Their latest rental car speared through the blackness of yet another highway, through pines so thick and deep Shawna had to wonder what was out there lurking behind them. Every once in a while her head lolled back against the seat. She was tired enough now that there were little aches in her joints, and her limbs felt heavy. The rhythm of the car's wheels over asphalt was a little hypnotizing.

"Close your eyes," Gabriel said. "There are no awards for heroism in this game. At least nothing you can take away with you."

She didn't believe that. She rolled her eyes to the side to look at him. "Then why are you doing it?"

"Not for the trophy."

She was afraid to go to sleep. Afraid that she would miss something—not so much masked gunmen running them off the road, but something that should have occurred to her by now, some piece they were missing.

Parts of this, she thought again, just didn't compute.

"If I were going to set somebody up, I wouldn't advertise it. I wouldn't give them a chance to get out of Dodge before the bullets started flying."

"Your point?" His voice had a certain rough edge to it. She realized that if she was exhausted, then he must be ready to drop. She didn't think he had slept much this morning when she had. He'd been at the window, after all, when she'd woken up.

"Why did that Apollo guy call us?" It was the question she kept coming back to.

"To keep us in that room for a few more hours."

"No, Gabriel. That makes no sense. We would have stayed if we *hadn't* gotten that call."

"Reynold didn't know that."

"Of course, he did. He had to figure we'd come to New York, hole up someplace and call him. It doesn't take a stretch of imagination to figure we'd spend the night." She paused. "I don't think Reynold did what you think he did. I think the killer got wind of our plans somehow."

He'd reacted to that phone call, Gabriel thought, with emotion, with anger, with his pulse pounding so hard behind his eyes that for a few moments he'd been unable to see. And that had left very little room for sense and logic.

So he listened to her, frowning.

"The killer didn't know that we set it up so that

you would call Reynold. Maybe he just figured out where we went and why. He kind of blew his hand, didn't he? Jumping the gun—so to speak—with having that guy from Apollo call us. He thought he was giving us exactly what we were there for. Instead, he was tipping us off."

"Shawna, *somebody* had to tell him what we were up to in order for him to do that."

But not Reynold, she thought. It just didn't feel right. "Call him. Feel him out. You know, see how the conversation goes. Just…see how he acts."

Gabriel knew with a sinking sensation that he would probably humor her. Eventually. If nothing else, he thought, she wouldn't shut up about it until he did.

"There's something else."

"Hmm?" His eyes were starting to feel grainy. It was becoming difficult to focus on the road. He couldn't go much farther. But that presented a plan.

"I think you should really consider this business about the D.A. That's been bothering me, too."

He took his eyes off the highway for a second to look at her, coming back to the conversation. "That's been my point all along. Something's wrong there."

"Something's *really* wrong. Your car exploded after you started pointing out in print that the D.A.'s office had the wrong time of death, and that they weren't interested in hearing about it. Maybe *that's* who decided you'd lived long enough, not Julie's killer."

"You think the D.A. tried to kill me?"

"They seem pretty driven to convict Stern. You could have foiled that, if you'd have stayed alive."

No, he thought. "That car bomb convinced me

even *more* that Stern wasn't guilty. Because he was already in jail, and he had everything to gain by me stating publicly that they had the wrong man.''

''Well, the D.A. couldn't have known that you'd live through it only to get more determined. And with you dead, it was one more thing they could pin on Stern.''

They hadn't actually charged Stern with killing him, Gabriel thought. They'd charged him with masterminding it—but no accomplice had ever been indicted.

''I'm just saying that maybe we ought to explore all the options,'' Shawna went on.

When, he wondered, had she had time to think of all this? She'd been running just as fast and hard as he had.

He'd been mulling it over for six months—and he hadn't seen a lot of what she'd just pointed out. Gabriel thought of that old expression regarding forests and trees. He wouldn't blow off her perceptions. She was coming into this with fresh eyes—as she had promised she would in what seemed like a lifetime ago.

''Get some sleep,'' he said again.

''You think I'm crazy.'' Her voice was disconsolate.

''Actually, yes.'' He paused. ''But maybe not about the D.A.'' And maybe not about Reynold, he thought, but he would have to give that one some more thought.

They were quiet for several more minutes. The dog let out a moan and snapped her jaws. Then she curled more deeply into Shawna's lap.

"Sweet dreams, pooch," Gabriel said. "Bite one for me." But when he looked over again, he realized that neither Belle nor Shawna had heard him. They were already dozing.

Chapter 11

Shawna roused just as Gabriel turned the car off the highway and onto a narrow road that dipped so suddenly it left her feeling queasy. But then, when it rose again onto the crest of a hill, the sky finally seemed to be a little more gray than black.

Dawn. Shawna lowered her window. The air had a bite to it, part of it cold, the other part pungent. Trees rose around them. In the relative dark the branches still appeared winter naked, but she thought that once the sun came up they would be tinted with green. New growth, she thought. Fresh chances.

"What are you doing?" Gabriel asked.

"Praying for a second wind."

Guilt squeezed at his heart. "We're almost there."

"Where, exactly, is there?"

"A bedroom and assorted other rooms tucked against the side of that mountain."

She felt disoriented—before she'd dozed, she was

pretty sure they'd gone north, south, east, west, in quick succession. "Are we still in New York?"

"Yeah. That's Schunemunk Mountain. It's near the town of Kiryas Joel." He felt her watching him and knew that he owed her some kind of an explanation. "The place was Julie's."

Shawna sat up suddenly. "Then it's an obvious place to look for you."

"Yeah. We'll hide in plain sight." Gabriel let out his breath. "We're being hunted, Shawna. I don't know where else to go now."

California came to mind. But his tone was so worn, she didn't have the heart to express any more of her fears. Shawna settled back against the seat again.

"My files are here," he went on. "The answer's in them. As soon as I find it, it won't matter where we are. We'll be safe again."

The sky was lightening steadily. He turned the car onto an even more narrow road—hardly more than a path that gave onto a driveway of scattered stones. After bumping along for another hundred yards, they came out into a clearing. And the cabin waited for them.

His first reaction was more guilt. He'd let the place go. *Hard to come up here and maintain it while I was dead.* But he hadn't made the drive in the months before he had died, either. So the cabin had waited, moldering. With its curtains drawn, it seemed to hunch in upon itself in a slow act of dying. But life thrust up from between the stones—weeds and grass and one enterprising vine that had crawled over from a nearby tree.

"It was pretty once." Did he sound defensive?

Shawna nodded politely. Then, once again, she hit

the nail right on the head. "There's fifty feet of open ground to the tree line on every side."

"Yeah."

"Kind of hard for anyone to get across without us seeing them. Unless we're asleep."

"There are motion sensors. They blink lights on if anything moves."

Shawna thought that as on edge as Gabriel was, that would probably wake him.

She pushed against the car door and got out. Belle roused on the seat, her head popping up, her habitual growl finishing on a squeak.

Shawna carried one of their bags to the porch. Gabriel brought the others. Then he put their bags down and cracked an elbow against the glass of one of the windows. Shawna cried out, jumping back when it shattered.

He picked the glass out of the narrow frame. When it was clear, he turned back to her. "Here's where you come in."

Shawna nodded. There was no doubt that she was smaller than he was. She lifted one leg over the sill, then reached for his shoulder to brace herself. She brought her other leg through until she was sitting on the edge.

"Damn," Gabriel muttered. "I was kind of hoping you might go in headfirst."

What a view *that* would have been, she thought a little giddily. And then she lost her breath for a moment.

She looked over her shoulder at him. He was halfway smiling. Her pulse quickened and she felt a dangerous degree of hope.

From the moment he had kissed her, something in-

side him had shut her out. I can't give you anything,
he'd said in the hotel suite. And his eyes had said, I
won't. But now, she thought, here was actually a little
innuendo. Maybe he was just punchy from their long
trip.

And maybe he was being honest.

Shawna finally looked away from him, but her
heart kept up a skittish pace. Leaning backward, she
slid through the window, into Julie's home.

She looked around. You have him for now, but
when this is over, he's mine.

Shawna pressed a hand to her eyes and nearly
groaned aloud. She was talking to a dead woman.

"Were you planning on letting me in?" Gabriel's
voice drifted through the open window. "I know
where the chocolate chips are."

Shawna's weariness drained away. In its place
came a voracious hunger that she hadn't been aware
of. "You've got *cookies?*" She went to the door and
threw back the locks. "Welcome home."

It had been the wrong thing to say.

He flinched as though a headache had suddenly
slammed into him. Then he stepped carefully inside.
"It was never mine."

And it hadn't been, he realized, looking around for
the first time in more than a year. He'd only been
here—what? Half a dozen times? Julie had usually
come here alone. To get away, she'd said, to unwind.
She'd bought it long before he'd known her.

"The cookies?" Shawn said hopefully.

Gabriel brought himself back to the moment. "I
lied."

Her face fell so completely he felt like a heel.

"Sorry, but they've probably gone back to dust by now."

"That long?"

He hadn't been here since Christmas—the Christmas *before* Julie had been killed. The murder hadn't happened until May. He'd spent last Christmas in his tired room in Philadelphia.

Julie, however, had been here two or three weeks before she had been killed. And she hadn't been planning on dying. So, he thought, there might be something canned, tinned or frozen that would have survived the interval. Maybe, looking toward summer, she'd laid in some supplies.

"Let's look in the kitchen."

Shawna beat him there.

What they found, given their starvation diet of the last two days, was a relative smorgasbord. The refrigerator was gruesome. Food *did* disintegrate, Shawna discovered. There were plastic-covered foam trays, straight from the grocer's refrigerator case, with absolutely nothing inside but green dust. The labels told her that they had once held Portabello mushrooms and veal cutlets. What remained of the veal was gooey.

But the freezer—ah, the freezer, she thought. *That* was a different story.

"Steaks," she breathed, almost moved to tears.

Gabriel's own mouth watered. He'd kill for a baked potato and salad. What they found instead was freezer-burned asparagus. He found a trash bag and tossed it inside.

But for as long as the killer left them alone, they wouldn't starve. He counted a pork tenderloin, a few more packages of filets, and something that might have been chicken.

What the hell had Julie been doing up here to need so much food?

"Surf and turf!"

He turned to see that Shawna had dug a tin of smoked oysters from the pantry. "There's wine." He joined her at the pantry and plucked out a bottle of good Cabernet. "But I'm fresh out of city lights."

Her eyes softened, almost misted. "Thank you for that. I never had the chance—"

Suddenly, he was angry. "Stop it. You've given up your whole damned life for me!"

She blinked. "I did?"

"The bar exam—"

"But I told you I wasn't going to take it."

He turned to face her with the wine in his hand. "No. You never said that was definite."

Shawna frowned. She hadn't, actually. She'd implied it. But she hadn't known until this precise moment that that was the choice she had made.

"I'm not going to take it," she repeated, to taste the words. "I just...can't."

He didn't censure her. He didn't berate her or try to change her mind. "What are you going to do instead?"

The thought of being a waitress for the rest of her life nearly brought her to her knees. The thought of going home to Kansas was even worse. "I don't know yet."

Then he touched her again.

He did it, she thought, when she didn't see it coming. This time, all he did was place a finger beneath her chin. But it had an effect on her, left a curling feeling in the pit of her stomach. He lifted her face until she had to meet his gaze.

"You didn't decide because of this." And his eyes said, Please say I didn't do this to you.

Shawna shook her head. "No. It's for the reasons I said in the car."

"Personal injury suits and tax loopholes." He moved away again. He looked over his shoulder at her as he uncorked the wine. "Well, with any amount of luck, we'll have some peace and quiet here and you can think about it."

"It seems more important to figure out who killed Julie."

And that, he thought, he *had* done to her.

He poured glasses and held one out to her. Shawna hesitated. It was six o'clock in the morning, he realized. Maybe that had something to do with her reluctance. But, hell, their internal clocks had been turned upside down for two days now. What, really, was the harm?

"What if they come for us? We should be alert, Gabriel, on our toes. Ready to run."

Ah, he thought, understanding. "Well, they will. They'll come for us." There was no sense in lying to her. "But not in the next few hours. We can't even be expected to turn up at Apollo until eight o'clock at the earliest." He took her hand and placed the glass of wine into it.

"How far are we from the weapon store?"

"About two hours."

She frowned. "We drove all night."

"Mostly in circles."

"Ah." She thought about that. "Ergo, we're safe enough for a minimum of four more hours. Actually, it will be a fair bit longer, because they'll have to figure out where we *did* go when we don't show up there.''

Gabriel grinned. He couldn't help it. ''Ergo? What's that? Lawyer-speak?''

The light didn't quite go out of her eyes, but it faded. ''It's hard to shake.''

''Just think about it, Shawna. Think about the bar exam if we have some time here.''

''I'd rather see your files.''

His grin faded so abruptly it hurt his face.

''No?'' she asked. ''Is that a no? Gabriel, I'm *in* this. It's kind of late to be arguing that fresh-eyes theory. What's the point?''

There wasn't one. And his reluctance was not something he entirely understood himself. ''I'll make dinner. Or breakfast. Whatever meal it is our bodies are expecting.''

Shawna watched him turn away from her. And she thought she understood. His pursuit of this killer was all for Julie. He wouldn't share it, wouldn't share *her*, not even if it would save them.

That hurt. It hurt deeply.

She took her wine and carried it back to the broken window. The cool dawn wafted in, chilling her. She listened to Gabriel moving about in the kitchen. Cabinet doors banged, then there was the clang of something metal that must have been a pot or pan. She closed her eyes briefly, trying to will herself back to sanity.

She could *not* be in love with him. So why did it hurt so badly that he *still* wouldn't let her in, not completely?

She sipped the wine. After two days with very little sleep, with even less food, she felt it hit her blood in an almost physical rush of warmth. She turned away from the window and looked at the room.

"So who *were* you?" she whispered aloud. "What were you like, to have such a hold on him?"

Julie had been attractive, certainly—Shawna had seen enough of her photographs over the years not to dispute that. She'd been beautiful in an exotic sort of way, and that brought an edgy feeling of purely feminine jealousy. Men had paid fortunes for the honor of having Julie grace their runways.

But during Julie's life there had been other pictures, too—scandalous ones, those that had been maybe not so attractive. Standing topless on some trendy bar in Manhattan. Ducking into a limousine, her face haggard, looking old after a rough night.

Shawna could not, for the life of her, envision Gabriel with a woman like that.

He had personal integrity. *Honor.* And he was far, far too controlled to have walked that wild side with Julie. In fact, she thought, she had *never* seen his face with Julie's in any one of those seamy-side photographs.

Which didn't mean they didn't exist, she reflected honestly. It just meant that she hadn't seen them.

And yet…she looked around the sitting room again and realized that it was subdued, tasteful, warm. Two walls were of glass, looking out onto the lightening woods. There were two white sofas, and a glass-topped coffee table. The carpets were Wedgewood-blue, along with a decorative throw over one arm of a sofa. A wood-burning stove sat on a plate of gleaming marble.

It was a *good* place, Shawna thought. It was a place that invited one to sit down, relax and enjoy the heat of the fire, surrounded by simple and calm elegance. Clearly there had been two sides to Julie. And one of them would not let Gabriel go.

"Come eat."

Shawna jumped a little at his voice. She looked down at her wine. It was empty.

She wandered into the other room, looked at the table there and found she could still laugh. "Gabriel, you are a creative soul."

What he had done with the food they had found was magnificent. Each plate held a grilled filet and a few of the tinned oysters. He'd found angel-hair pasta. She sat and took a mouthful of it, then a piece of the steak.

In a gourmet restaurant, it would have earned a review that closed the doors. There was a stale freezer taste to everything. But given their lives these past couple of days, it was heaven.

"Olive oil and garlic powder," he said of the pasta. "There's no butter. That's all I could find."

I'd marry a man who could do this. "You can cook," she sighed. Life was looking a little less appalling.

"Now, see, you wouldn't have struck me as the type to fall into those gender stereotypes."

Shawna widened her eyes deliberately. "Did I say anything about gender?"

"You didn't have to."

"Gabriel, I'm a woman, and I can't cook to save my life."

He realized he was surprised. He'd begun to think she could tackle anything.

"I don't like it. Life's too full to spend hours simmering at moderate heat."

She must have read a recipe or two, then, and had decided that the whole process wasn't to her liking. He ate more steak. And he realized he was relaxing. In spite of everything, the wine, the food and her company seeped under his skin and warmed him.

"I married Julie when I was twenty-six," he heard himself say, "so there were a few bachelor years before then. I like to eat."

"So you learned to feed yourself. And the skill lingered."

"No. The skill got perfected out of necessity. Julie didn't cook, either."

Shawna frowned. "So what was she doing with all this food?"

It was a good question, one he still couldn't figure out.

Shawna finished and pushed her plate away. With her stomach full, she could have fallen asleep with her head on the table. But Gabriel was suddenly restless.

He got up and poured them more wine. She thought about demurring, but he wasn't with her just then, she realized, looking up into his face. He'd gone somewhere far away, and he was hurting.

"I didn't know her," he said finally. "We were strangers those last months. Maybe even the last years."

Shawna reached for her wine after all. She sipped and opened her mouth to respond, then she shut it again slowly.

No, she thought, this wasn't the time for cheerful platitudes, either.

"Did you ever read how I met her?"

Shawna thought about the question, about what it

revealed. Not did I ever tell you, but did you read it? Because, in large measure, he had lived his marriage in a fishbowl. They'd both been famous, in their own ways.

"No." She shook her head.

"I was still a cop. And Julie was modeling. Some fan was stalking her. The NYPD bent over backward to protect her. You don't want celebrity blood spilled on your turf."

He realized what he had just said. He winced, and Shawna felt briefly cold.

"Anyway, I was assigned to the case. And I was bowled over by her. They put me on the scene, by her side, twenty-four hours a day. I had to move in with her. For four weeks. It was a big penthouse on the upper east side."

"Gabriel," she said, wondering, "were you as taciturn then as you are now?"

"I'm not taciturn. I make my living with words."

"But you don't *speak* them freely. You never say what you feel." She saw by his face that he didn't like the assessment. "It's just an observation."

Still, she could almost see it. A younger, earnest Gabriel, grimly determined to do the very best job. And Julie...Kovar, she remembered suddenly. Yes, that was what her maiden name had been. She would have been vibrant, burning bright.

Complete opposites.

"She was like a firecracker," Gabriel went on, as though reading her thoughts. "The trouble is, they go up, and they're beautiful, flaring, shooting colors, but they're always cold by the time they hit the ground."

He put his wine down and leaned his palms on the table. Sort of like he had a lifetime ago in that coffee shop, she thought, when he'd told her he had an obligation.

"What did she *want?*" he demanded. And Shawna knew he wasn't asking it of her. "Her whole life was a frenzy. Everything about her was on the edge, except when she was here in this little house." He straightened again, running his hands over his face briefly. Then he left them there for a moment, looking out at a day that was becoming blue and bright.

"Whatever it was," he said quietly, "I never gave it to her. And that killed her."

"No." Shawna was on her feet in an instant, facing him down.

"I was always too driven, chasing my own pursuits. Writing. Digging. Understanding other people. Never my own wife."

"*Could* you have?" Shawna cried. "Could you have understood her? You were too different. Different people get married all the time. Sometimes it works. Sometimes it doesn't. But most of us don't end up murdered so the other party has to take on some self-denying, gargantuan task to atone for it!"

"I owe it to her, damn it! If I had gone with her that night, she'd still be alive!" There, he thought, it was out, spoken. The words rang through the airy room. They flayed something inside him.

"No, Gabriel. You'd be dead, too."

"You don't know that."

"And *you* don't know that it would have worked the other way around."

She didn't understand, he thought. So he would tell her. "We *fought* that night. The reason I know Julie was alive at nine-thirty was because we were *arguing.*"

"There's a hanging offense."

He came closer, anger beating behind his eyes. "Don't do this to me."

They were both too tired, she thought. Too frightened, too tense, too desperate. And she let the words out, anyway, fighting words. If she could make him see what he was doing to himself, then she *knew* he'd be better off for it. "What...? Call you a fool?"

Gabriel left her suddenly. He went to the door and flung it open so hard it cracked against the wall. Shawna made a sound of distress and went after him. She saw through the glass that he rounded the corner of the house, then he came back with one of the boxes they'd sent up earlier.

His files.

He threw it on the table. It skid and hit a plate, sending pasta over the edge of the table and making glass shatter. He grabbed a folder and flung that down as well. The top flipped open.

And there was blood.

Shawna gave a sharp little cry. She had never before seen what she was looking at now, the brutality, that gruesome shredding of life. All the food she had just eaten pushed up into her throat.

"You want to see my files?" he demanded. "You want to be my fresh eyes? Well, there you go."

He was being cruel, she thought. But then, she had dared to disparage his guilt.

Deliberately she pulled her eyes away from that top photograph. "Gabriel, you did not take that knife to her. Someone who hated her did."

He blinked, as though seeing her for the first time, as though she had materialized out of nowhere. "What did you say?"

"*Hatred* did that. Your only crime was indifference."

Gabriel sat down at the table again, and he did it hard.

Was that what he hadn't been seeing? He had been going at it clinically, factually, sorting through black-and-white data for six months. But he hadn't looked, hadn't really looked with his heart *and* his eyes, because he couldn't bear to see.

Shawna had. She'd seen the truth in an instant.

"A fan?" she murmured. "Could it have been?"

Gabriel reached across the table and closed the folder again. His voice croaked. "The physical evidence doesn't point to that."

Shawna sat down, as well, gingerly. Still not sure of his anger, but willing to go that one more step. To save him, she realized. To pull him back, before it was too late.

Maybe *that* was why fate had tossed her at him. To make him see and set him free. Even if she also lost him in the process.

"Gabriel, don't die for it. You've shriveled up spiritually. You're a hollow shell, with only vengeance to keep you going." And you're shutting me out. "Whatever guilt you feel about Julie's death it can't be so all-consuming that you throw your life away."

He could have spoken the words again. I owe her. He believed them with all of his soul. But they hadn't impressed Shawna.

Shawna watched his expression turn inward—again. The fight drained out of her. She got to her feet.

"Where are you going?" he asked harshly.

"To find someplace to sleep."

Damn her if she thought she was going to tear apart everything he'd spent months living by, then walk away. "Get back here!"

"You don't want me, Gabriel. You'd don't want to hear what I have to say. You'd rather embrace your guilt."

He stared after her.

It was subtle, a certain shifting in the chemistry between them, but he felt it strongly. He was losing her somehow, her faith and her belief in him—things he had never earned in the first place.

She had given them, all the same, freely.

Gabe, that damned book will still be there in the morning!

He winced as Julie's voice came back to him again. What had he said to her that night? He scrolled back through memories. *I've got an obligation.* The words rang eerily in his mind. That time it had been to his publisher. He'd been behind schedule on that book.

Come with me, Gabe. Please. Just this one time.

He'd said no.

She'd thrown something then. A vase, maybe a glass. And then she'd gone, slamming the door behind her.

A cracking sound brought him back to the present. Shawna had found the bedroom, and she'd shut the door, as Julie had shut another door nearly a year ago.

It was Julie he owed, because he had already turned his back on her. Another obligation. But, God, he was so tired of toeing the line.

Gabriel stood from the table and went down the short hall. He put a hand on the doorknob, then he pulled it back again.

Do the right thing. Why did he always feel that

compulsion? Because his parents had instilled such a sense of responsibility in him? Easy, he thought, to blame others. And too easy to overlook the big picture.

He'd been a cop once, a good one. Then he had spent six years going after justice in a unique and different way, giving victims a voice, letting the world know how and why they had died. It was what he did, what he'd always done. He righted wrongs. And always he put that first.

You tackle things, Shawna had said.

When they need tackling. And as long as he didn't decide that something else needed tackling more.

There was a right way to do things, he thought, and a wrong way. He'd always strived hard to be right, so he could live with himself. Was it right to leave her in there, angry, hurt and alone, after all she had given him?

He put a hand on the knob again. But this time the door opened from inside. Shawna flung it back—and stood like a firebrand on the other side.

Here was the temper he had only glimpsed before.

"I want to finish this," she said heatedly.

Her eyes were nearly black with storm clouds. Her cheeks were flushed. Her hair was wild as though she had been thrusting her hands into it. Without warning those hands came up and drove into his own hair. Tangling strands between her fingers. And then she kissed him hard.

She drew back. "Don't you dare make my choices for me!"

He was dazed. "I'm not—"

"You *are!* You're trying to. You have from the

start. And unless you honest-to-God feel not the slightest attraction to me, stop it right now!''

"For God's sake, I never said—''

"Do you?''

"What?''

"Feel the slightest attraction to me?''

How could she possibly believe anything else?

"Okay, then. Stop pushing me away.''

"There are reasons—''

She snarled. *"Stop.* Don't you *dare* decide for me that I'm not going to have this because it's safer or saner or more virtuous or...or whatever your reasons are. I could *die* trying to help you unravel this mess. That's what you keep telling me. That it's dangerous. That it's deadly. Well, I'm here, Gabriel. And my life is on the line, too. I'll be damned if I'm going out of this world without being with you, without *experiencing* you, even once, just because it's the right, safe, sane, virtuous thing to do!''

His mind stopped with the word *experience.* "Is that all?''

"No. This is.'' Then her mouth was on his again. Hungry. Avid. Something furious and edgy and desperate exploded inside him.

He thought she cried out when he lifted her off her feet, but his blood was roaring in his ears and he couldn't be sure. Yes, she'd provoked him.

His mouth found her breast through the cotton of her T-shirt. That, too, was unlike him. He wasn't an animal. He'd always preferred finesse. But this time he tackled what he wanted, without judging and weighing first.

He reached the bed, and they fell together upon it. *"Experience?''*

"Please," she whispered, and something snapped inside him.

He dragged the T-shirt over her head. No bra, but he had known that since encountering that scrap of lace dangling from the shower in his apartment. His hands covered her breasts, finally touching her. "Is this what you want me to do?"

She whimpered. "Yes. Touch me."

He was damned.

She was made for this, he thought suddenly, for good, hard loving and a long, wild ride. He'd known that from the start, too. There'd be no simpering, no coyness with her, just energy. It came off her skin now like heat.

Her breasts were small, their tips hard from his mouth, and he closed his lips over one again. *Experience.* He threw the floodgates wide, letting out the storm of everything he had held back against for so long.

Pulses seemed to shoot through her wherever his mouth went. They left every nerve ending raw. Shawna pulled at his shirt and heard her own voice pleading. If she had been waiting for this time, with this man, all of her life, then the last few days had been the hardest.

Flesh to flesh. She dug her fingers into his skin and tried to bring him closer. She couldn't stop herself from demanding, because she knew she might never have this same chance again.

Slow it down. Savor it. Treasure it. But she couldn't.

It was like before, when he had kissed her. He wanted her with a reckless urgency that was unmistakable. So she dared to believe again that this Gabriel, this man who dragged her jeans down her hips impatiently, who streaked his hot mouth over her skin, this man might want her enough to stay when the running was over.

A dangerous precipice there. But she let herself fall over the edge.

"You should have left when you had the chance," he growled.

"I couldn't," she gasped. "It wasn't supposed to be that way. And someone had to believe for both of us."

The words, so simple, so uniquely her, shattered his willpower as much as anything.

His hands needed to be everywhere, on her pebble-hard nipples, beckoning to him, on her hips as she writhed to his touch. He wanted to give her an *experience* that would make her ache with pleasure whenever their eyes met with the memory of what had happened here tonight.

She lifted one leg, ran her calf against his hip. Parting for him, ripe and willing. Without guile.

And Gabriel knew he felt alive, exquisitely and completely alive again, for the first time since Julie had died. He needed. He craved. She'd given him that, and she gave more, as she had from that first moment she'd smiled at him.

He held himself back again, but this time he did it because cherishing her became suddenly so important.

He let his mouth roam until need was a scream in his head and his hands shook. He used his teeth and his tongue until she began twisting beneath him. Then she clawed his jeans off.

Mind-numbing hunger, she thought. Something

within her had been reduced to a being without thought, without pride or rationalization. She wrapped her legs around him. Then she shifted her hips and took him in. And the sensation of him filling her was hand and glove, a perfect fit, the way home.

Gabriel watched her face, and what he saw there was pleasure unhidden, a smile unabashed, a heart so pure it shook him. And knowing that, knowing it had always been there for him, he let himself thrust into her hard.

She moved in perfect counterpoint against him. He watched the climax slam into her first. Even as she groaned with it, he kept on, bracing his weight on his arms. Her nails dug into his shoulders as she held on to him. He caught her hips and held her, pumping. That was when she tipped her head back, her throat arched and vulnerable, and gave herself over to the way he made her feel.

Gabriel felt something explode inside him, everything he'd thought he knew about himself. He did the wrong thing for all right reasons, and he lost himself in her.

Chapter 12

It was dark again when Shawna awoke. She swam to the surface, her body clinging to the rest it had craved so badly. She felt pleasantly stiff and sore, pleased and utterly languid. She smiled dreamily and turned over into Gabriel's warmth beside her.

He made a sound deep in his chest and pulled her closer. Since he was asleep, he did it purely unconsciously, Shawna thought, and her heart swelled. This, and the way he had loved her earlier, told her everything she needed to know. When his defenses were down, he wanted her. And that was enough, for now.

She snuggled deeper into his embrace and woke him. Gabriel groaned.

"Don't be sorry," she said quietly. Anything but that. She waited for him to say something, anticipating something that might hurt, her heart thudding.

"Well," he said finally, "it wasn't my fault. You started it."

She let out a strangled sound that was half laughter, half relief. "Spoken like a schoolyard bully."

"That was you. I was the overwhelmed ninety-pound-weakling."

This time she laughed purely. "Not even close."

He chuckled, then the moment was lost. He sat up against the headboard, taking her with him, but something had changed.

"What time is it?" he asked.

Shawna still wore her watch, though she couldn't see it in the dark. She reached to turn on the bedside light. They both squinted in the sudden glare, and Shawna sighed.

"Ten after nine." They'd slept a solid twelve hours.

"I guess they've stopped expecting us at Apollo by now."

It doused her mood. Shawna slid her legs over the side of the bed. "Can we hang up the posters? I want to see them now that I know what I'm looking at."

Gabriel hesitated. But he couldn't say why.

Everything she'd said from the beginning had proved true. Her fresh eyes had seen things he'd been staring at dully for months now without recognizing.

Let her look at it all, he thought. See what she came up with. It made every bit of sense in the world. So why did he have this sense that he was betraying Julie?

The answer came quickly and uncomfortably as Shawna rose from the bed, naked. He cherished the curve at the small of her back, the slight and narrow but athletic build of her. With a breath, he felt himself

stir, ready to love her again. Then she dragged the
sheet with her, wrapping it around herself, but his
own reaction didn't go away.

It felt like the utmost infidelity to allow Shawna,
of all people, to unravel what had happened to Julie.

Across the hall, he heard water begin to drum in
the shower. Gabriel got up and padded naked into the
sitting room and found their bags. He got clean jeans
from his tiny duffle and stepped into them. He collected their money again, then recounted and stashed
it. Finally, he went outside and he brought in the rest
of his files.

When she came out of the bathroom, Shawna
stopped quickly in the main room and looked around.
All the boxes were inside, piled up against one wall.

Her eyes flew to him. He was going to let her help.

She knew better than to thank him, to say anything
other than practical words. So she crossed the room
and picked a file. "I'm hungry."

"You won't be if you start with that one."

She realized it was one with pictures. She put it
down again quickly.

"Where are…I don't know, things like circumstantial evidence?"

"The time lines and graphs are all on the posters.
I'll tack them up after we eat. Those files over there
are full of interviews and whatnot."

He went to the kitchen.

Shawna took a file into the sitting room, and she
curled up there on Julie's sofa, in front of Julie's
wood burning stove, and she read about the last hours
of Julie's life.

There were interviews with friends, with family
and, of course, with Gabriel.

Why didn't you go with her?

I had to work.

Make any phone calls? Did you go anywhere? Or were you alone the entire time?

My God, she realized, they'd suspected *him.* How could anyone who knew him ever think such a thing? Her flesh crawled briefly as though ants had traveled over it.

Gabriel's lawyer had objected to that line of questioning. He had answered, anyway.

I called my editor.

When?

Right after she left. At about 9:35.

His interrogator had skipped right over that and had gone on.

Shawna frowned, flipping back a few pages. The interview had taken place seven days after Julie had died. It had been conducted by the NYPD, not the D.A.'s office. Had even the *cops* not cared that the time line was wrong?

Something queasy settled into her stomach. She went back to where she had left off, and read on.

There were interviews with friends who had expected to meet Julie and Talia at a club that night. But, of course, they'd never shown up. Those same friends had been asked about any unsavory characters the two women might have been involved with, and they had staunchly insisted that there were none.

But Shawna was not naive. She *knew* what went on with that high-wire kind of existence. Gabriel had to know, as well. Had there been drugs involved? If drugs were involved, where had they bought them?

Shawna looked around the sitting room again, frowning. The woman who had decorated this place had not lived on the edge. But there was a jagged line down the middle of Julie's two personas, with rough edges, like a piece of paper torn in half.

"Hungry?" Gabriel asked, jolting her.

Shawna sighed and put the folder down. "This didn't ruin my appetite, but it gave me a headache."

"Nothing ruins your appetite." But he knew the feeling. "I found some aspirin in the medicine cabinet."

She went that way first and swallowed a couple.

When she came back to the kitchen and looked at the table, she gave that smile he was beginning to crave. "Damn, you're good."

Gabriel grinned wolfishly.

It hadn't been easy, he thought, sitting across from her. If they were going to stay here much longer, they would have to risk going out to a store. The nearest town was six miles away, and it was a small one. But there would be bread and eggs there, the staples.

The best he could do for a meal was something vaguely like soup. Canned broth, more pasta, some spices and the chicken filets he'd found crusted with ice at the back of the freezer. Shawna dug in, anyway. God bless her.

He waited for her to come up with some startling insight from her hour with the file. He *expected* it. For days now, gems of wisdom had slid from her tongue with little or no provocation. What could she do now that she was actually trying?

Apparently nothing. Or, at least, she wasn't ready to talk about it.

"So whodunit?" he asked when he couldn't stand it any longer.

"Well, it wasn't your butler."

Gabriel surprised both of them with a bark of laughter. They hadn't had one.

Shawna finished the soup, sat back and sighed. Then she grinned at him a little lopsidedly. "I'm sorry. I'm not *that* smart. I need time. I need to read all of it first."

And preposterously, in that moment, he knew that he loved her.

It made no sense. There was no connection between what she had said and the sudden heat that flooded him, that stunned him. But what about any of this had made sense from the start?

It was the way she looked so genuinely abashed for having failed, when all she had done was try to help him. The way her eyes turned inward at the end of her smile as her mind already went back to picking at what she had learned. It was her absent stroking of the dog as it jumped up in her lap and the way her gaze slid to his own soup.

"Are you going to eat that?"

"Uh…what?"

"Are you going to finish your soup?"

Gabriel shook his head. "No. Go ahead."

She got up and put it on the floor for the dog.

He'd been going out to make a phone call the morning of the mugging, he found himself thinking. Just a phone call on another grim, tense day. And there she'd been. He'd watched her dragging that dog about. It had been a curious sight, so it had snagged his attention. But he had not been able to take his eyes from her. And then that boy had struck.

He remembered how thoughts of her had haunted him even after the mugging. Maybe she was right.

Maybe they shared some connection he could neither name or explain.

Maybe she'd been meant to turn his world upside down.

"Shawna."

She came to her feet again. Her smile lingered, but it was uncertain now.

Of course, he could not say the words. And the reasons were all the same ones that had kept him from touching her for so long. He did not know how they were going to come out of this. He had something to do first, before he could promise her anything. And she was a woman who deserved promises.

He couldn't say the words, but he could show her. He'd already crossed that line.

Gabriel stood and held a hand out to her. She came to him, putting her hand in his, frowning now.

"What? Is something wrong?"

"One more time," he murmured. "Can I have one more time?"

He could have all the rest of her time. Shawna pulled her hand free when she understood what he wanted, and she rushed at him.

The impact of her body made Gabriel take a step or two back. He bumped up against the table. "I need you." It was the closest to an admission he dared to give right now.

The words filled her, bright as promise. "I'm here," she whispered, rooting for his mouth again. "Oh, Gabriel, just let me be here for you."

She had never left him, he thought, not once, except for those hours when he had sent her away.

With a sound that might have been pleasure, that might have been pain, he went for the zipper of her jeans. Dragged them down. She leaned her weight on one foot to accommodate him. She wore panties this time, and he cursed soundly.

He hooked a finger beneath them at her hip, tugging. His mouth worked down her body, starved for her. He shoved at her T-shirt—she wore a bra this time, too. He got rid of it. The taste of her skin, clean and sweet, pale and smooth, inflamed him.

He would not think of the contrast with Julie. And with that one quick flash of thought, he no longer did.

He let himself sink into everything that was Shawna. Unabashed energy. Life pulsing just beneath her skin. Goodness. Hope. And that certain unique, mind-boggling craziness.

The air kissed her skin. She was chilled and hot. Instantly aching, and amazed. She had not expected him to want her again so soon. His defenses, she thought, so sturdy and strong, like everything else about him, had gone back into place the moment they'd left the bed. She did not know what she had done just now to break through them, but she said a profound, silent thanks and gave herself to him.

His jeans. They had to go. He'd never put a shirt on. That was good. They grappled with each other, each wanting more, and the table skidded on the hardwood floor.

"Here," he said.

"Now." And they agreed on that.

He cupped her bottom and slid a finger between her legs and heat beat there, almost pain. Then he lifted her, turned, and she wrapped her legs around his hips as he settled her on the table.

He was so hard and deep inside her. Sensation took her, and she let it. She looked up into his eyes at the moment she toppled over the edge, and she saw something there she would gladly die for.

Afterward they sat at the table, talking about nothing and everything.

"Maybe a social worker," she said about her decision regarding the bar exam. "I already have the education for that."

His brows went up. "No fine wine and three-hundred-dollar shoes there."

"They were a fringe benefit."

"Parents who don't give a damn about their kids? You'd be miserable. People aren't always good, Shawna." More often than not, they weren't, he thought.

He was probably right. "Scratch that avenue."

Then she thought suddenly, treacherously of doing *nothing*. Of being with him like this through lazy idle days when they *weren't* running. She could bring him sandwiches and soup while he was working. Maybe she'd even learn to cook.

That shook her. What was he doing to her? She'd never been the kind of woman who was content with being idle. But there was a part of her now that wanted to spend her days just…being in love with him.

She thought—for just a moment—of children. Her sisters all had passels of them. She'd decided long ago that they were something she'd prefer to postpone. Until she had her law degree and her city lights. Until she'd tackled the world and all its problems.

But as she watched him get up and go to tack up the posters, something new and undiscovered inside her yearned. For days like this, end upon end. For dark-haired, blue-eyed children who would know—as she did—that this man was worth the world.

Shawna got up quickly and pushed the thoughts away, shaken by them. She took another file to the sitting room. She fed a log into the stove and buried her nose again, doing what she was good at. Half an hour later, she realized he was gone.

Shawna put the file down and went to look for him. He was facedown on the bed. Snoring. That made her smile.

She leaned over and touched her mouth to his temple, and for a moment, just a moment, something panicky moved inside her again. Because there was nowhere she'd rather be than here, and she knew she could lose him in a moment.

She could lose him to a monster. She could lose him to memories of a woman who was gone. She could lose him forever.

But first, she was going to save him.

She straightened and looked over her shoulder, out the window. Were they coming yet? Had the killer figured it out yet, that Gabriel had, in a respect, come home?

She went back to the files, because doing something was far better than sitting and fretting. And by the time Gabriel came into the sitting room again, just past five in the morning, she thought she had something.

She didn't sense him at first. She was too engrossed. It was the scent of him that roused her, the one that had first come to her after the mugging. Spicy. Warm. Home.

Shawna looked up. "Hey," she murmured. Any more words than that were beyond her. He stood there, still only in jeans, his hair mussed and ruffled. Bleary-eyed. His hands in his pockets. And the sight of him touched everything she was.

"What time is it?" he asked.

The question of the day, she thought, or maybe of the night. But, of course, they were both thinking now of how many hours had passed since they'd been expected to appear at Apollo.

"It's almost dawn," she said.

Gabriel sat down. "So it's pushing twenty-four hours now since we didn't show up."

"Yes. But I found something that might help."

He looked at her sharply.

"Maybe it's nothing," she warned.

"Hit me with it, anyway."

"It's just something else that jumps at me because it doesn't make sense. You know, like why anyone would call us in the hotel room."

His eyes continued to warn her off the subject of Reynold. Okay, she thought, so he wasn't ready to call his friend yet. Shawna nodded slowly. "I've gone over all the physical reports, everything that Reynold and Bobby sent through the post office boxes." He probably wasn't going to like this, either. "It's that DNA thing."

Gabriel felt his heart jump. "According to that information, it's Stern's DNA."

"So where's the physical report?"

"What?"

"The data. You know, one of these." She picked up another file on the other side of the sofa. "You've got lab reports and all the coroner's reports. The neat, physical stuff you were warning me away from, as opposed to the circumstantial."

"Bobby gave me that DNA report over the phone."

"Okay." Shawna pressed her fingers against her temples. "But everything else like that he sent on a paper copy. So why? Why not send the DNA report that way, too?"

"Maybe the D.A. didn't release anything in print."

"But why wouldn't they?"

"They don't always do that for the public, Shawna."

"Well, Bobby's not public, right? He's a cop."

That quelled him. Yes, there should have been a physical copy of that report.

Gabriel felt that quickening in his gut again, that certainty, that if he could figure out the DNA glitch, he'd know it all.

"Let's say it's accurate," she went on, picking her words with care now. "Let's say that the DNA under Julie's nails does match Stern. I know a little bit about DNA, Gabriel."

He didn't answer. She thought he looked braced for a blow.

"For criminological purposes, what they do is compare a person's DNA to a test group of ethnically like individuals, and they derive their ratios from that. So...if you throw someone's kin into that test group, it throws the whole thing off."

His heart was slamming. It left him with a faint feeling. "We're talking about 23 chromosomes."

"Yes."

"Offspring would share half of each parent's."

"It was an extra course I took once when I had a little money. I thought at one point about going into criminal law."

No jokes about high heels and wine this time. He looked at her, and her expression was dark and troubled. "So what you're saying is...that I should distrust Bobby also."

"No, Gabriel. No. Just...let's get that physical report if we can. There's a chance I could make some sense of the data. Why just take anyone's word?"

He shot to his feet.

"Where are you going?"

"I want to look at the time lines again."

She followed him into the living-dining area. He went to the photo of John Thomas Stern's only child, a son by his first marriage.

John Thomas Stern, Jr.

The man's face looked back at Shawna, slightly arrogant, with a strong nose, but undeniably handsome. Shawna guessed him to be in his early thirties. Stern, Sr., was sixty-six. And Talia, his much-younger second wife, had been his son's age.

Julie's contemporary, she thought. They'd formed a strange, neat little clique.

She scanned down the time line. "He was in Paris. So I was peeling off in the wrong direction."

"Not necessarily. He bought a plane ticket to Paris. I have those records somewhere. And it was used. But anyone could have been on that plane, in that seat."

"So where does that leave us?"

"I've got to find out for sure who flew out of La Guardia that night." Maybe it had been Stern, Jr., he thought. Then again, maybe not.

He'd never followed up on it. He didn't know why. Maybe, he thought, it was the matter of that forest and those trees again.

And maybe it was because he had blindly accepted

Bobby's word. Bobby had dug into the details of that flight for him, he remembered. His stomach went rock hard for a moment.

"You can't find out, Gabriel," Shawna said. "You're dead."

"What?" He focused on her again.

"Let me do it. If you start snooping around, asking questions—"

"No." Something happened to him. And it was physical. A quick rush of nausea—that was part of it. His temples pounded.

"Joe Q. Public doesn't know me," she persisted. "The fact that I'm asking questions would stay quieter longer. If you start moving about the streets of New York, it will cause an uproar."

"I said no!"

There was no rational explanation against it. It was all in his gut. Denial. Absolutely not. Fury at a faceless enemy. Leave her out of this. None of which, he thought, were necessarily rational or sane under the circumstances.

He left the room. Shawna watched him go. For the time being, at least, they had time. And she was determined to convince him.

She went back to the files and picked up the first one she had seen, the one that had flipped open on the table when Gabriel had brought it inside. She looked at the top picture again. Julie was curled, almost fetal-style, on the pavement. But her throat was arched, open, laid bare. Shawna shuddered, felt her gorge rise again, but she looked. She *kept* looking this time.

At Julie's hands, curled like claws.

At her opened eyes—betrayed and knowing.

At the way her dress was torn and her legs were scissored.

Shawna's breath started coming fast. She dug deeper into the folder for more photographs, not wanting to see them, having to.

Talia Stern. She'd died on the steps leading up to the door of the brownstone. As opposed to Julie, she was simply…asleep. Lying on her back, one arm splayed, the other crossing her waist. There was a look of mild surprise on her features. Her eyes were closed. There was only a solitary slash to her neck, neat and directly on target.

No hatred there, Shawna thought instinctually. Talia's was just a necessary death. But the fight Julie had waged for her life had been livid, vicious, one of slashing emotion.

She went back to Stern, Jr.'s, time line. To his somewhat unsubstantiated trip to Paris. It was probably nothing. A tiny thing, or Gabriel wouldn't have overlooked it. But she got the file that bore Stern's son's name, anyway.

She'd already scanned it once, and it had left her vaguely surprised. Now she *read* it, word for word. It was full of police reports. Drunk-and-disorderlies, mostly. Here he'd been standing on the roof of a high-rise, stark naked, swinging around a flag pole. In this one, he'd had a brawl with someone he'd deemed to be a homosexual. Nothing overtly criminal, she thought. Nothing that had waved a red flag, for either her or Gabriel. It was just more parties, life on the edge—fast, faster, fastest.

Like Julie. Shawna's stomach clenched.

She looked at one of Stern, Jr.'s, psychiatric reports. It had become public record through the process of an expungement hearing stemming from one of his bad-boy charges. Mild alcohol dependency—he could control it if he tried. And the drugs she had wondered about before—there was some usage, she saw. Which made his bizarre brushes with the law all the more unremarkable.

Then the last paragraph caught her attention. ''Patient suffers narcissistic delusions. Patient craves attention.''

''Gabriel,'' she said hoarsely.

There was no answer. Of course, he'd left the room, angry with her, or at least not willing to listen to her.

Craves attention...

The words leaped around in her head. What, she wondered, would a psychiatrist have said about Julie?

''Gabriel!'' she called again. An inner voice was cautioning her. Don't say anything yet, wait, go check out those airline records first. This was such a long shot, nothing but a hunch, really.

Still, it made so much sense. They'd been two peas in a pod. Friends, after a fashion. At least contemporaries in the same wild world. Two needy people.

And it would explain the DNA.

Gabriel had gone down the hallway. Shawna went to the bedroom they had shared just hours ago. He wasn't there. But something was different, something that made her pause and frown. A photo that should have been on the dresser was gone.

She was sure it had been a publicity shot of Julie. They'd done something with electric fans to make her hair flare, Shawna remembered. Her eyes had been slits, contemplating, come-hither. Chin tilted up. It had been cropped above her chest, but the implication was that she had been naked.

Patient craves attention. "Oh, God."

She went into the room, to the dresser. She touched a finger to the blank spot. Then she turned about. Her heart stopped, started, then stalled all over again.

Gabriel was in a garden room off the bedroom, sitting on the edge of a hot tub. Holding the picture.

Julie's picture. The one that was missing from the dresser. Well, Shawna thought almost dispassionately, it had to be that one. And she knew in that moment, looking at his expression, at his eyes, that he was not ever going to leave her.

Hopelessness was deep and liquid inside her. It even swam into her bones. She made a small sound in her throat. Please, no, don't let it be this way.

But she had known all along.

She had just been too stupid—no, too *naive*—to accept it. She thought of the way he had pushed her away in the beginning. He'd only made love with her because she had demanded it. Because she had thrown herself at him, wanting so very much for him to touch her.

To want her back. But he wasn't ever going to. Not really.

She'd deluded herself that his loving had meant something. But, of course, she had given him little choice in the matter. She knew in her heart that if she hadn't pushed it, he would never have touched her.

He'd run, he'd denied, he'd remained one step removed from her from the first moment of their acquaintance. And she had recognized that, on some level, because she had been afraid of her growing feelings for him. She had been afraid of *this*.

As she watched, he traced a finger over Julie's photograph, and his mouth moved.

He was talking to her. To his beloved, lost Julie.

Shawna clapped her hand to her own mouth to keep from crying out. Then she turned away from the garden room, from the sight of him, and she fled.

Chapter 13

Gabriel had picked up one of Julie's publicity photos, but he might as well have taken one of those with her throat cut. It was how he had remembered her now through all the months since she had died.

Still, this photo seemed more appropriate. Arrogant, hungry and needy, this shot had captured the real Julie. This was the one to whom he needed to say goodbye.

Who had she turned to, who had she smiled at, in those last days to appease her ego? he wondered again. Stern, Jr? Someone who had *hated* her had opened Julie's throat. And that same someone was fighting for his freedom now. For the right to go on with his life, with no one the wiser. He would kill again, Gabriel knew, if it meant saving himself.

"You had one, you bastard. *One*. That's enough. It's too damned much."

It had to end here, he thought, and yes, denial rose

in him. But the decision also felt right, as right as Shawna's breath against his chest when they'd woken, when she'd thought he'd still been sleeping.

It was, of course, the ultimate betrayal of Julie. Much more vicious than refusing to fawn over her beauty or gallivant by her side during her life. It was what Gabriel had always sensed that Shawna's involvement would come down to.

He was going to have to walk away from his obligation now.

Gabriel waited for fresh anger, because Julie had deprived him of something he desperately needed and something he deserved. Right or wrong, he took his obligations seriously. And yet...he wasn't angry.

He was afraid. He was terrified that something would happen to Shawna, maybe the same thing that had happened to Julie.

Gabriel put the photo down on the rim of the tub and stood to pace, thinking.

There were roughly thirteen thousand dollars left of that old woman's money. He had—*used* to have— cash in his New York apartment as well. They could disappear for a while.

Bora Bora came to mind. Someplace with thatched huts far, far away, removed from the world in both culture and miles. The living would be abominably cheap, and they'd grow bored long before they'd be able to return safely. But they'd return alive.

How had Shawna put it? It was time to get out of Dodge. Gabriel nearly smiled.

Instead, he gripped the last of the bottle of the wine he'd brought into Julie's garden room. He looked at her photo again.

"You wouldn't have wanted anyone else to die,"

he said aloud. "You were wild and you were hungry, but you were never cruel."

There was no answer. Of course there wasn't. Julie was long dead, even in his heart, except for the rancid guilt she could still stir in him.

Gabriel paused, thought about that. "I ran from her at first, you know. Because I knew she would do this, with her hope and her light."

Had he ever, in thirty-six years of living, *run* from a woman? Not once, not twice, but three times? Four, he thought, if you counted that midnight hour when he hadn't gotten away. Of course he'd known. He'd known that somehow she would change everything.

"Even when I let her in—when I had to—I gave myself excuses and ground rules," he went on aloud. "I wouldn't let her get too close, wouldn't let her attract me, because I needed all my wits about me to keep us alive. I sure as hell wouldn't touch her, because I owed you this quest. Because I wasn't there eleven months ago, so I was damned well going to be there now. I wouldn't let her help, because this was something I was giving you and that would sully it, would spoil it somehow. The answer had to come from my efforts, from *me*." Gabriel took another swig of wine. "I was denying the most important thing, the biggest reason I tried to keep her from getting too close. I couldn't fall in love with someone else on your time, the last time I could give you."

He waited for a thunderbolt to come down from heaven, one flung from Julie's own manicured, slender hand. It didn't happen.

"I won't breathe another breath without wondering who did this to you. I won't sleep another night without demons. But I've got to get her out of here. I've got to keep her alive.'' If the killer took Shawna, too, vengeance wouldn't be enough. The truth of that left him both hot and cold, all the way down to his bones. Too much of him would die with her, with this woman who was so extraordinarily convinced that their paths through life were somehow intertwined. It was that part of him that had just come back to life.

She'd made him laugh again.

Gabriel put the wine down and left the garden room. He went into the bedroom, shutting the glass doors carefully behind him.

He half expected to find Shawna there, sleeping again. She'd been up all night, and she wasn't one to thumb her nose at a good, well-deserved nap. But the bedroom was empty.

He went into the kitchen and found the bowl of soup she'd put on the floor for the dog. Belle had turned her nose up at it.

His heart thudded once, a little too hard, as he looked around the empty kitchen. ''Shawna?''

He went into the sitting room. Files were still splayed all over the sofas. But there was no sign of her.

He called her name more loudly, angry at her now for scaring him. But still there was no response.

Terror took over.

For a moment he thought it would literally knock his knees out from under him. He turned back into the hall and pounded a fist on the bathroom door.

Nothing. No one.

He didn't register that the little house show no signs of a struggle. He just saw the emptiness. He saw what he feared most.

She was gone.

* * *

The man was livid.

He sat ramrod straight in his desk chair, his hands like claws on the arms. The phone was on speaker because, he knew, he could crush the receiver now with his hands.

He wanted. And what he wanted, he always possessed. Only one man had ever thwarted him. And they'd lost her to that man. The imbeciles. Fools.

Beyond the crack in his drapes, dawn began to shine, with its treacherous fingers of rosy light and its insidious promise. It would bring another day of waiting, he thought, in a room shrouded from the light. Because he'd come to hate the day, when things happened, when people asked questions. He'd learned to cling to the night, when all was quiet, when he was safe.

He had not believed he would spend this dawn alone.

"Where is she?"

"Not far. Close," the caller explained hastily. "Julie's place, as a matter of fact, near Kiryas Joel. We've found them there."

Shock, fury and betrayal became a bright pain in his blood. What had she done?

They'd slid out from beneath the caller's nose nearly twenty-four hours ago. They'd never shown up at the gun store. And now they were here. There!

"I've already got guys in place," the caller said. "We'll move in as soon as—"

"You'll move in," the man interrupted in dangerously dulcet tones. "Yes, move in. Kill him. Do you understand me? Get rid of Marsden now. He can't have her. But keep her alive. And bring her home."

There was a short hesitation. "What do you mean *home?*"

"Enough. This is enough. I want her here. With me. Immediately."

The man gave great concentration to removing one hand from the arm of his chair. He reached out a single finger and gave a deadly punch to the phone, cutting the caller off.

He'd heard, of course, that killing got easier. And this, Marsden's death, was just…a snap of his fingers. No blood on his hands. Not this time.

He sat back in his chair, finally breathing more quietly, then he smiled.

Actually, it felt good. He liked it.

She would not cry.

What was the sense? Shawna thought, moving through the woods with Belle at her feet. She'd forced her way into this, into his life. She had no one to blame but herself.

He'd shown her, she thought again, had tried to tell her from the start. But she'd barged in, anyway, her heart blinded by hope.

She stopped in a clearing, giving Belle a pause to sniff through the winter's dead leaves. Each beat of her heart was a pained thud. She crossed her arms over her waist as though to hold herself together.

She could have loved him, she thought, her throat so tight she struggled a little for air. He was such a good man, strong and true, honorable and sure. Careful not to hurt, to cause pain. Doing the right thing, always.

Yes, she could have loved him. But his heart had

been slashed beyond healing eleven months ago. It belonged to another woman forever.

He'd died with Julie. She couldn't save him. Gabriel did not want to be saved.

"Shawna!"

At the sound of his voice, closer than it should have been, Shawna whipped around. Please no, not now. She couldn't face him now. Just hours ago she had been deluding herself about a future with him when this was over. Believing that how he touched her in moments of emotion was a start.

She needed time to pull herself together. She wasn't ready yet, would surely embarrass herself by pleading, or—God forbid—crying. Shawna turned back into the woods, hurrying now.

Then Belle barked as though to alert Gabriel to their presence.

"Whose side are you on, you little Judas?" Shawna stopped and tried to grab her. The Chihuahua danced away, then she hurtled into the woods.

Not in the direction Shawna was going, but back toward the house. Toward Gabriel.

"Shawna!"

There was a cracking sound in the underbrush this time. Finally, blessedly, something like temper reared up in her. It was far better to be angry, she thought, than to feel her heart bleed. She turned back. "Go away!"

"What?"

"Leave me alone!"

She saw him now, coming up the path. Then he stopped and they faced each other over a windfall of dead wood. The path ran around it. Belle scrambled up onto the heap of wood, wagging her tail, barking again.

"Are you nuts?" Gabriel demanded. "Are you out of your mind?"

"No. Not anymore. I just got it back again." Oh, *damn,* she thought, damn, her voice was cracking.

"So get reacquainted with it back at the house, why don't you? Or do you have a death wish?"

He was still angry at her, Gabriel realized. No, he was *furious.* There'd been that breath of relief when he'd first realized she was out here, safe, alive and unharmed. But the risk she'd taken inflamed him all over again. And now, here they were, standing out in the open, and she was acting…crazy.

Why should that surprise him?

But it did, he realized. It really did. Because through all the time they'd spent together, she'd actually been rational in her own unique and skewed way. He'd been able to make a certain sense out of everything she said or did. And that was the point. She always made it clear what she was feeling and why. But this…

Gabriel dragged in breath. What the hell did she have to be angry about?

"Come back to the house," he growled.

"No."

"No? *No?* What do you mean *no?*"

The breeze lifted that golden hair and flung it across her face. She reached up, peeled it away and crossed her arms over her breasts without answering.

"You want to let me in on this sudden mood swing?"

She turned away from him again suddenly and began running deeper into the woods.

Gabriel's heart froze a moment, then it picked up rhythm again—irregular and frantic. "Shawna, no, don't!"

Belle began barking crazily, a cacophony. Gabriel went after Shawna.

He was closing in on her—a mere three yards separated them—when the first gunshot rang out. The bullet pinged off a tree six inches to his left. If he hadn't jogged around a fallen log, it would have hit him.

Then the dawn exploded, shattering into a million broken pieces. There were flashes of odd, disjointed images he was sure he would remember for the rest of his life.

Shawna screamed at the sound of the shot and reeled back to him.

Gabriel heard his own voice ring out again. *"Get down!"*

Then the dog—that crazed, pint-size Goliath—leaped into midair, attaching her jaws to Shawna's forearm. Stopping her, Gabriel had a moment to think. And it worked. Shawna yelled and shook her arm to fling the dog away.

Another shot kicked up leaves between them. If she had gone down, as he had told her, she would have been right there.

Gabriel roared, a wordless sound. Belle finally let loose with her jaws, but now she was tearing back the other way, those little legs churning up leaves. Coming directly at him.

Gabriel tried to step around her, but she tripped him. He went down, catching himself on braced arms, as the next shot rang out where his head had just been.

Shawna's screams were ricochets now through the

forest. She reached him and flung herself down beside him. ''Oh, God, oh, God, did it hit you?''

''Run,'' he rasped.

''Not without you.''

God, yes, she was crazy. And she was his. She'd stay by him. He opened his mouth and knew it wasn't even worth fighting with her over it.

Belle yipped crazily, dancing in circles. Clutching each other, they got to their feet.

No gunshot this time. No gunshot. That meant something, Gabriel thought, but he couldn't think what it was right now.

They sprinted back through the trees together.

''The car!'' he shouted.

''We need the keys!''

''I've got them!'' They'd been on him, or near him, every moment from the time they'd arrived. Same with the money. Just in case.

Shawna reached the car and pawed at the door. When she got it open, Belle took the front seat in an airborne leap of three feet. Gabriel jumped in the other side, reached across, grabbed Shawna's arm, and hauled her the rest of the way inside.

She was still struggling to close her door when he peeled rubber, tires spewing stones, and backed at full tilt down the drive. The car bucked, veering.

''Oh, God, oh, God, oh, God,'' Shawna gasped.

''Stay down in case they shoot again.''

But of course, she didn't listen. Belle put her paws on the dash and continued to yip.

''Shut *up!*'' they yelled in unison.

At the end of the drive, Gabriel punched the brakes, sending the rental car into a skid, then he shot forward. They bulleted down the road.

Halfway to the highway, he noticed a reasonably new Dodge Ram. Empty, abandoned, bright red, and parked on the shoulder. Something about it made Gabriel's heart squeeze, but there was no time to think about that yet, either.

Belle had finally settled down. She was breathing hard now in sharp, little pants. Or maybe that was Shawna.

They were nearly back to the highway before she spoke again. "We were just about out of food, anyway."

Gabriel meant to laugh, but all that came out was a choked sound.

He kept the accelerator floored, driving hard. The gunmen would be behind them by now. Unless that had been their truck, he thought. If they'd had to run all that way for their transportation, that gave him a bit of a head start.

Something about that truck. He needed to think about it. There was a lot he needed to think about.

One thing at a time.

"What the hell possessed you?" he growled.

Shawna blinked at him. "Me? I didn't shoot at anybody!"

"To go out there alone!"

It seemed to him that she went still. Then she shifted in the seat uncomfortably. "Oh, that."

It was all it took. Gabriel felt crazed by temper all over again. "*Oh, that?* That's your only explanation?"

She gave him an almost haughty look. "Yes. For now." At least, she thought, with everything that had just happened, she was too rattled to give undue attention to her heart.

But it lingered. What she had seen still hurt abominably.

"Of all the lame-brained, imbecilic—" Gabriel began, but she cut him off.

"Stop."

"You owe me an explanation! You damned near got me killed!"

He was right in one respect, she realized. It *was* Gabriel who had nearly gotten killed. They'd been shooting at him, not her.

The realization was stunning. All along she'd thought they were after her, too, if only by association, because she was with him. But back there in the woods, most of the shots had been aimed at Gabriel. She wasn't positive, but it had seemed like that.

"I don't understand any of this anymore," she whispered aloud.

"Lady, that makes two of us."

She looked over at him. His jaw was grim, set hard. "What now?"

"Plan A is out."

"I wasn't aware that we had one." They'd been running for days, with no further purpose than whatever next stop Gabriel had chosen. And they hadn't yet planned for this eventuality. "What's Plan A?"

Impossible now. The words flared into Gabriel's mind and he bit them back. It had seemed so simple when he'd been alone in the garden room. Get out of Dodge. Bora Bora. Somewhere removed from civilization and from time.

But the killer wasn't going to let him go now.

Gabriel realized that they were the only people in the world who could stop this. It seemed as though they were the only ones who cared. It would never be over until they finished it. Running, hiding, would only prolong the nightmare. They'd *never* be able to come back, not until the killer was unmasked. And only they cared enough to do it.

The killer knew that, too. They were the last real threat to him.

Shawna didn't like the look on his face. "What?"

"We're going to the airport."

"To check on Stern, Jr.'s, alibi?"

"To send you home."

She had a physical reaction that was conflicting enough to be painful. A yearning to get away from the hurt he'd caused warred with denial against being cut out of this now.

She thought back to the woods. To that first gun-shot, when she'd thought he'd been hit. She'd known then, of course. Because in all of the chaos, even with Belle jumping up out of the blue and biting her arm, the realization had been crystal-clear and bright in her head. She *could* have loved him? Too late, she thought giddily. She already did.

It didn't matter how short a time she had known him. Gabriel was her other half, and she'd understood that from the first moment she'd looked up into his eyes. She would never be whole without him.

Yes, she thought, yes, the best thing to do was to get out of this now. To go home, lick her wounds, pick up the pieces. Put him behind her, this incredible, wonderful man who would never love her the way he'd loved his Julie. Go home, a voice inside her pleaded. But then another voice—the one of her faith, of her belief—said, Not until this is over.

"No. I want to finish this."

"It's not your choice to make." Gabriel's jaw set even harder.

So Shawna changed tactics. "What are *you* going to do?"

He took his eyes off the road for a second to look at her, surprised. "I'm going to do what I was always going to do. I'm going to find out who he is."

"Well, as long as we're at the airport, we might as well check Stern, Jr.'s, ticket to Paris. That might help."

He looked at her again warily. He knew how this went. She was being too agreeable.

She raised her brows at his expression. "What, you're going to shove me on a plane *then* go check the ticket?"

"More or less. You're out of this, Shawna."

The killer didn't want her, he thought. When they'd clutched at each other, when they'd run together, the bullets had stopped. Not taking a chance on hitting her? What the hell?

If he sent her to Kansas, Gabriel reasoned, what were the odds that the killer would divide forces to go after both of them? Slim, he thought, and it was a gamble he would have to take. It was the only way he could think of to protect her. If they split up, if they split wide, the killer would probably go after one of them or the other.

And, Gabriel thought, the killer seemed to want him more.

"I'll be back," he heard himself say aloud.

This time her expression was genuinely startled. "What?"

"I'll come back for you. When this is over."

"Why?"

Just like that, he thought, simple and sweet, to the point. It was so like her.

No promises. He would not offer hope if there was any chance that he wouldn't come out of this alive.

The way things stood now, she'd get over him. Weeks would pass, months would go by, and all this would begin to seem like a strange dream. Unless he told her he loved her.

He knew the woman she was, and with her loyalty, her faith, her hope, she would hold on to that for a lifetime.

For a moment, just a moment, Shawna dared to hope again. But with his silence that hope floundered and drowned one more time.

Shawna looked out the side window. Let him plan all he wanted. She had a few ideas of her own.

Chapter 14

La Guardia was as quiet as it ever got, which was to say that they made it all the way to the concourse without anyone stepping into him, pushing her aside to pass or trying to thrust religious pamphlets at them. Still, Gabriel was tense. This was going all wrong.

They'd had a heated argument at the ticket counter, which had effectively made her miss the first flight he had wanted her to be on. For some reason that he was afraid he could understand, Shawna had been okay with flying back to Philadelphia, but she was dead set against going to Kansas.

Of course she could get off a plane in Philadelphia, turn around and be back in New York less than two hours later.

"When it comes to my family, your wishes don't amount to a hill of beans." She shifted the dog until she was braced against her hip, little legs dangling.

It didn't matter. He had a ticket to Wichita in his pocket.

"I'm not going. I can't deal with them right now, Gabriel. When they find out what I've decided about the bar exam, they'll want me to come home for good. You have no idea what they'll do to me."

Ah, he thought. "You're still going. I have my reasons."

"Which are? Or are you too arrogant and high-handed to share them with me? What *right* do you have to just point me in a direction and think I'll go there?"

He felt his own temper tug. "I'm trying to keep you alive, damn it!"

"Then what's wrong with Philadelphia?"

Because from Philadelphia, she could come back, he thought again. Easily. And before this was over.

He stopped walking, and ticked off other reasons on his fingers. "This guy knows where to look for you in Philadelphia. His goons will be lying in wait for you. They'll grab you and try to find out where I've gone, what I'm up to."

"Where *are* you going?"

"That's my point! What you don't know can't be dragged out of you!"

"Well, if I'm not going back to Philly in the first place, then who's going to drag it out?"

She had a point, but this was going nowhere.

Gabriel tried one more time, patiently, sanely. "I don't think he'll have anyone follow you to Kansas."

Shawna deflated somewhat, too. She scraped her hair back from her forehead, shifted the dog into her arms, and looked glumly around at the crowd. "If it's distance you want, there's always Fort Lauderdale."

It was the closest she would come to admitting that Philadelphia was out.

"If you stay at a hotel in Lauderdale for any length of time, our money is going to get eaten up in a hurry. And I need the cash to keep moving."

"Where? Where exactly will you be moving to?"

She didn't give up. *Ever.*

He had three more hours to withstand her pleas, because the next flight to Wichita didn't depart until noon. "Let's get something to eat," he said, to distract her.

"I'm not hungry."

Gabriel stopped again and swore.

"Well, I'm not," she said indignantly. "Don't get testy about it."

"You ate stale chips in my apartment! You ate that soup I made! What I know about you is that you will eat anything, anywhere, at any time!"

"That's not true. For instance, I really lose my appetite when I think about going back to Kansas."

He wanted to throttle her. He wanted to hold her, to draw her close, to smell those sunflowers and know that she was safe from harm for always and a day. He took her arm and steered her into a nearby bar.

He plunked her deliberately at a table, but then he stood beside it as Belle settled down in her lap. "If I tell you my plans, will you eat something?"

She shrugged. "Maybe I could. Just don't mention Kansas."

So he sat. And he ordered them burgers. It occurred to him that he had never tasted anything so perfectly delicious in all his life. Shawna devoured most of hers, but she fed small, unobtrusive bites to the dog half-hidden under the table. Then he watched her mop up ketchup with a French fry. He'd been right. Eating kept her occupied for awhile.

"There's no sense in checking on that plane ticket," Gabriel said finally. "Bobby already did that. I was dead. He asked around for me."

She thought about it. "You're saying that the only prayer we have of proving Stern, Jr., wasn't on that flight is if someone saw him here while he was supposed to be *there*."

It was exactly what he planned to work on, once he got her safely out of harm's way.

"When, exactly, was his flight?" Shawna reached for the rest of his fries now. "I don't remember."

"The day before Julie was killed." Which was part of what had made him close a mental door on Stern, Jr., in the first place.

"So if it's him, it was premeditated. He planned the flight, made it look like he was out of the country, so he could actually stay here and kill her." She paused. "No, Gabriel, that doesn't work."

"Why not?" He wondered, with a pang, where he was going to be without her insights.

"I saw those pictures. That wasn't a cold and calculated murder. That was some kind of *frenzy*."

Gabriel rubbed his forehead. Damned if she didn't have a point.

"Unless there was some other reason he wanted people to think he was away from New York at the time."

Gabriel dropped his hand quickly. "Such as?"

"I don't know." Then, abruptly, she stood again, gathering up Belle. "Come on. I've got an idea."

"Wait—"

But she was already cruising out of the bar. Gabriel

threw some bills on the table to cover their tab and went after her.

"Let's call him." Her eyes began scanning the concourse for a pay phone.

"What?" He caught her arm. "You're nuts. Do you know that?"

"Actually, Gabriel, I think maybe I'm the only one seeing this sensibly right now. How much time do you think we have left?"

He didn't answer. It was a miracle that those Dodge Ram shooters hadn't gotten here by now. But maybe they'd lost them. Maybe this was the last place they'd expected them to go.

Shawna leaned back against the wall, clutching the Chihuahua. "In just a few days, this has escalated, gotten crazier and more dangerous and more wild with each passing minute. Gabriel, now they've tried to shoot us. So do we even have the rest of today to nail this guy? He may kill us both by nightfall."

Gabriel couldn't answer. It was too true, and any words he might have spoken got caught in his closed throat.

"What if we died, Gabriel, what if we both died, and left this unfinished, let him get away with it all?"

There was such fierceness in her eyes, it hurt him. "Justice," he muttered.

"Yes. It would be like killing Stern, Sr., too. The D.A.'s going for the death penalty. Think about it. Julie. Talia. Me, you and Stern, Sr. Are we going to let this guy get away with all that?"

Exhaustion hit Gabriel in an overwhelming rush, not a physical draining so much as a mental one. "Shawna, we have no proof, not one shred of it, that Stern, Jr., was involved."

"It's in my gut."

She said it so simply. And he believed her. Still, he felt compelled to be rational. "You just said back in the bar that it couldn't be him because his alibi was too calculated."

"No. I said he didn't buy that ticket to France for an alibi."

What the hell was the difference? "Why, then?" He asked it quietly, almost afraid to hear her reasoning.

But now that she had the opportunity to tell him, Shawna found the words stuck in her throat. Because if she was right, the truth would hurt him.

She had a flash of him in that garden room again. Her heart squeezed. Incredibly, and against all her willpower, tears gathered in her eyes. She blinked them back hard and turned quickly to the side to hide them.

Given what she had seen with him and that photograph, she knew that what she suspected would devastate him. And she couldn't do it, couldn't tell him, couldn't hurt him that way.

No matter that he couldn't love her. She loved him. It was that simple, that powerful.

"There are reasons," she said finally. "Things I've thought of. There's not a lot of time to tell you now. Can't you just trust me on this?"

He would trust her always, forever, intrinsically. He wondered if maybe she wasn't the first person he had *ever* trusted, because it was simply beyond her capacity to be cruel.

"So you just want to call him up and—what? Just outright accuse him?"

Shawna nodded. Unbelievably, she nodded.

Gabriel rubbed his temples. "No matter what he says, Shawna, it's not proof. I can't go back to Bobby and the D.A.—who thinks I'm full of garbage to begin with—and say that Stern acted odd when I accused him of murder."

"No, but we could tape the conversation."

"You're out of your mind." But he thought about it. And the idea began to take shape. He could set up a meeting with the guy. And yes, he could tape what was said. His mind started working, playing at it, then he noticed a man in a Mets cap walking slowly down the concourse toward them.

He was glancing left to right, Gabriel noticed, then back again. He had both hands in his jacket pockets. Cold ants trailed over the knot of tension at the back of Gabriel's neck. "Come on."

"Do you see someone?" Shawna looked around a little too wildly as he pulled her away from the wall.

"Maybe." Who knew? Did it matter? Could they take the chance? "Let's find a telephone."

The man waited through the sunlight.

It was full day now, blue-and-white light streaking in through the crack at his drapes. Cruel light, revealing light, that tightened his nerves into painful coils.

He tried to remember when it had changed, when he had started hiding from the sun.

It had happened when—beyond his belief—they had taken his father. After weeks of terror, of a constant heart rate so brisk it left the man dizzy with every move, after weeks of blood on his hands and rage and grief in his heart, they had taken his father. He'd been reeling over what he had done—such real trouble this time and something that had shredded his soul. And then they had charged John Thomas Stern, Sr., with the crimes.

Stern, Jr., had known in that instant that he was saved. All he had to do was get through this trial.

The jury was seated. The proceedings would begin on Monday. And once it was over, once his father was incarcerated, everyone would forget about Talia and Julie. Appeals took lifetimes. If Stern, Jr., could wait until a conviction, *survive* that long, he would once again have his own life to enjoy. People would forget.

Until then he avoided the daylight. He went out at night. He had to go on normally. And normal, for him, was a round of socializing, of being out and about, night after night.

He had stayed out of trouble. Not one skirmish, not one tangle with the law, in eleven months. Because they couldn't look at him, couldn't even glance his way. They couldn't be permitted to wonder. And something had happened to his system after Julie had died, anyway. No matter how much he drank, it seemed he could no longer get drunk.

Sobriety had a cunning grip on him, forcing him to remember every moment of her dying, freezing him into eternal awareness of every second that passed while he waited for the trial.

It all hinged on the DNA.

Julie had taken pieces of him. He'd known that from the moment he'd watched her eyes go opaque, when he'd known he'd lost her. He'd had the scratches for weeks. Of course, they thought it was his father's blood. His father had had a few unfinished scores to settle with Talia. Everyone thought that she'd been the target, that Julie had walked in on it.

The man let out a bray of nervous laughter, then he rubbed his hand over his mouth. His mind veered.

Where were they? Where was his caller? He should have heard from him by now. Invariably, when he did not hear from his caller for a long time, something had gone wrong.

He blinked. His mind jumped again. Why hadn't Marsden just stayed in that apartment? It had looked, for a while, like he would do that indefinitely, until long after the trial was over.

The man went to fret with the drapes again, trying to shut out that sliver of light. Then he returned to his desk to stare at the phone. Where was she? Where was his caller?

And then, incredibly, as though he had willed it, the telephone rang.

He snatched it up from its cradle. "Where is she?"

And at the airport, in a phone kiosk that offered neither of them any real protection, Gabriel reached out to draw Shawna closer. His blood went instinctively cold.

"What?" Shawna whispered. "What's the matter?"

Gabriel placed a hand over her mouth. And for once in her life, she quieted.

"Who?" he said into the phone in a neutral tone. Then he waited for Stern, Jr., to realize that the voice that answered him was not the one he'd anticipated.

They'd met a handful of times over the years. Gabriel wondered if that would be enough for Stern to recognize his voice. Probably not. On all those occasions they'd been in a bar or at a club, with voices straining loudly over screaming music. They'd had nothing in common—Gabriel hadn't cared for the man—and their conversations had been minimal.

No, he realized in the next moment, Stern did not know who he was speaking to.

"Who is this?" the man demanded.

Gabriel waited a beat. Then he bluffed. "I know. I know everything that happened."

He thought he heard a mewling, unstable sound on the other side. Then the line clicked off.

Gabriel put his hand out. Shawna shoveled more change into it. "My God, Gabriel, did he hang up on you?"

"Yeah. One more go-round."

"I was right!"

"Either that, or he's out of his mind on general principal. Or cocaine. He's paranoid." The ringing on the other end of the line broke again and Stern's voice came back. "Hey," Gabriel said. "We got disconnected. And I was just starting to enjoy this conversation."

"Who is this?"

"I'm your worst nightmare."

"Marsden."

His name, spoken like an epithet, rewarded Gabriel. He glanced at Shawna and nodded to let her know that it was going reasonably well. Then Stern, Jr., effectively whipped the rug right out from under him.

In a heartbeat, everything changed. Everything he'd planned disintegrated like dust.

"Where is she?" Stern, Jr., demanded. "Where's Shawnalee? Did they take her from you?"

A sense of vertigo hit Gabriel, as though the entire

airport were dipping and twisting. Shawna? "What about Shawna?"

At the sound of her name, she jerked in his arms.

"I want her. You have her. We'll make an exchange."

Gabriel pulled the phone away from his ear and stared at it in dull amazement. What the hell was happening here?

He put the phone back to his ear. "For what?" he asked carefully. "You don't have anything I want."

"Oh, but I do. I can tell you why." Stern's voice changed, going silken and wheedling. "You want to know, don't you? Why Julie died? You want to know it all. You want to know how it was. That's what you've been doing, isn't it, all those months in that seedy room? You want to know how the blood of her life pulsed out over my hands."

An admission.

After so many months, so many nights alone staring at his files, here it was. No fanfare, Gabriel thought, no trumpets blaring to announce the truth. Just the blood of her life over my hands.

Through all his searching, thinking, striving, he had never guessed.

Shawna had known.

Gabriel made a thick, guttural sound he wasn't aware of. Shawna grabbed the phone out of his hand.

"What about me?" she screamed at Stern.

There was a pause of surprise. "Darling, you're still with him? Why?"

Her head swam. Her skin tightened over her bones. She knew, in that moment, that they were not dealing with anything sane.

Shaking, she thrust the phone back toward Gabriel.

He didn't quite catch it. But he saw through the haze of his fury that her face had gone white.

He felt his own physical reaction recede. "Ah," he said quietly, and pulled her closer. "Easy, lady. Easy does it."

The phone dangled at the end of its chain. Stern's voice squawked at them, but distantly.

"I can't do it," she whispered. "I'm sorry. I can't talk to him."

"It's okay. It's all right. Of course you can't. What did he say?"

"He called me darling."

Gabriel stared at her for a moment, then at the phone.

Not just Julie now. Julie had made her own choices, had lived her own life. Shawna was in this for him. Because of him. This, he thought, was war.

He grabbed the phone again. "Stern! Are you there?" There was a sound. Not a reply. "You want to trade?" You sick, twisted bastard.

"Bring her."

"I will. Oh, yeah, I will. But I want to know. Every detail."

"Yes." Stern giggled. Gabriel's flesh crawled.

"Meet me—" He grabbed Shawna's arm, looked at her watch. "At eleven o'clock. At your father's theater. The one near Forty-third."

"That's closed now." He sounded peevish.

Gabriel hung up the phone without answering.

Some color had come back into Shawna's face— not much, but a little. She tried to rally. "Okay. Come on, let's go."

He felt none of the old terror claw up in him. There was no nausea this time. No panic. It simply wasn't going to be. She was not going anywhere near John Thomas Stern, Jr.

"Shawna. You're not going."

She stared at him a little blindly.

He took her hand. Sometime during the past few days, he had finally learned to do that, to touch her, easily. Without measuring, weighing, coming to the decision. She'd taught him. Now it was too late to enjoy it.

He turned up the concourse again. She went with him—this time, she followed. He took the plane ticket from his pocket as he approached the first gate they came to.

He looked at the sign there. Milwaukee? It would have to do. The plane was leaving in ten minutes.

Yes, he thought, somewhere in this nightmare there was an angel watching over them. He stopped at the counter. "I want to exchange this for a ticket on this flight."

The woman looked up at him, startled. "We're boarding now."

"Good."

Shawna still stood quietly. Too quietly. He looked at her. Either she was exhausted or stunned, or both, but she seemed out of it.

He slid the Wichita ticket across the counter. The woman began tapping at her computer keys. "You have a twelve dollar credit."

"Keep it." He turned back to Shawna and took the dog gently from her arms. Belle snarled a little, then settled down.

"Shawna. Get on the plane."

"I can't go to Milwaukee. I don't have any clothes."

He stared at her. Ah, he realized, he wasn't thinking at all. He was just keeping her alive. And it hurt.

He dug into one of his pockets for some of the
money. After the cost of her plane ticket, he had
something like twelve hundred dollars in that roll. He
gave it to her.

She'd get off in Milwaukee and use it to find a
plane back to New York. He knew that. But by then,
it would all be over.

"Ma'am, we're boarding. Are you actually going
to do this?" the woman asked.

"Of course, she is," Gabriel snapped.

"Gabriel, no—"

"Get on the plane before it leaves without you."
Then, breathing deeply, he added, "Shawna, Stern
wants you."

She recoiled. "But why?"

"I don't know." He would find out, or he would
die trying.

"Ma'am—"

"She's coming."

"No, I'm—"

So he pushed her. He got behind her and put his
free hand on her shoulder. He propelled her toward
the boarding ramp.

"Gabriel! I can't just—"

He pushed her a little way into the tunnel and
backed away.

The woman smiled at him a little crookedly. A
lover's spat, her eyes said. Too bad, so sad. Gabriel
turned away.

"*Stop!* You can't do this to me! You—" Then Ga-

briel heard the sound of the ramp door closing. It cut
off her voice.

His breath left him. He felt like a bullet had found
him, after all, squarely in the chest. He missed a step.

Then, without looking back, Gabriel walked on.

Chapter 15

"There you go. Right there." The stewardess stopped midway down the aisle.

Shawna flicked a gaze at the seat, at the woman, and it took her eyes a moment to focus. "I'm going to Milwaukee."

"Yes, that's right. After a quick layover in Columbus. It should be no more than half an hour."

Milwaukee? Columbus? What was happening here?

Shawna dropped into seat 12 C. She was on her feet again in an instant. "No."

The stewardess turned back to her. "I beg your pardon?"

"No! You don't understand. Or maybe you do. Have you ever loved someone?"

The woman frowned. "I'm married—"

"There then! You have!" The engines changed

tone. She had to go. "Please. I've got to get off this plane."

The captain's voice broke in over the speakers, warning that they were about to taxi to the runway. Shawna panicked and ran to the front.

The stewardess moved quickly behind her.

"I love him. And if I don't get off this plane and go after him *right now,* I'm never going to see him again. It's…it's a feeling I have. This isn't right. This isn't the way it's supposed to be. And—he has my dog!"

"I'll—uh, talk to the captain," the stewardess said.

"*Please.* Hurry."

Ten minutes later, the stewardess still hadn't come back. But the plane hadn't left the gate either.

When the woman finally emerged from the cockpit, she opened the door and Shawna flew into the tunnel again and up the ramp.

Gabriel would have left the airport by now. Or he would be in the process of leaving it. He was—what? At least ten minutes ahead of her, she decided. She'd never catch up to him before he got to the car. So she'd have to take a cab.

She ran along the concourse until her lungs burned. Take a cab where?

To the theater. They were going to meet at a theater. On Forty-third. Forty-third and *what?* Broadway, she decided. It was the only thing that made sense.

She burst through the terminal doors onto the street—and straight into John Thomas Stern, Jr.'s, arms.

She only knew him from a flat photograph. Yet when he caught her, when she looked up into his face,

she recognized him instantly. She knew him in her
bones.

And he knew her.

How could he know who she was, what she looked
like? It was incredible, preposterous, unless it had
been him personally on their trail all along. But Stern
seemed as startled to find her as she was terrified.
Shawna screamed, jerked away from him and ran.

No, no, God, no!

She realized she was begging people incoherently
as she passed them. A few of them hesitated to look
at her.

Why does he want me? And then she heard Gabriel's voice.

"Shawna!"

It was a roar of rage—and yes, she heard the disbelief there, too. She stopped and searched wildly for
him in the throngs of people streaming up from the
parking lots.

Then Stern, Jr., barreled in on her from behind.

He tackled her, knocking her legs out from under
her. She went down hard, and her forehead cracked
against the pavement. A sense of déjà vu gripped her.

Not this time. This time she could not pass out.

She fought him. But he was strong, and not as frantic and unsure of himself as that mugger had been.

"Don't run from me," he gasped. "Why? Why
would you run from me?"

Shawna screamed and writhed to get away from
him, trying to buck his weight off her. Then she felt
the knife at her throat.

Her breath stopped, half-suspended in her chest.
And she knew—God help her, but she knew—that it
was the same knife that had killed Julie.

They'd never found it, because Stern, Jr., had had it all along.

"Did he have you?" Stern said.

"What?"

"Were you with him?"

She didn't know what he meant. But she knew that the longer he talked, the more surely Gabriel would reach them.

So she opened her mouth to respond. Then, without warning, Stern's hand was in her hair. Pain screamed over her scalp as he hauled her to her feet again. The knife was gone—too briefly—then it was back again. And this time she felt the sting.

He'd cut her. The edges of her vision started going black. Shawna fought the sensation off. She'd be damned if she was going to pass out every time some-one hurt her. She squeezed her eyes shut, then opened them again.

And then she saw Gabriel stop, no more than ten feet from them now.

"You lose," Stern, Jr., said, giggling. "No trade, Mr. Marsden. I have what I want. And you'll never know."

Gabriel roared and charged them. Stern reared back, dragging her with him. He cut her again, a gouge when he moved and tightened his hold. Shawna let out a strangled, terrified cry.

Gabriel came up short at the sound. Stern, Jr., laughed again shrilly.

"Don't come closer. He'll hurt me," she said in a voice that was too frail. Did Gabriel even hear her?

"She's right, you know," Stern said cheerfully. "It's just like Julie. If I can't have her, you can't, either. Stay back, Mr. Marsden, or I'll kill her right here. You can even watch this time.''

Then Stern was dragging her backward, one hand still in her hair, the other holding the knife at her throat. And Gabriel could make no move, not without Stern killing her. The crowd stood frozen, gaping at them, before a person here or there rushed off.

''You're coming with me now,'' Stern said in a whisper against her ear. ''Don't worry, darling, we'll get this straightened out. I won. I always win. You'll see that.''

Shawna shot Gabriel one last pleading look. *I'm sorry, so sorry. For not staying on the plane,* she thought. *For being so stupid.* She dragged in breath, and every piece of her heart shattered.

Her fear left her. She could not care about Stern. She cared only about the man who was watching Stern drag her away. Because the look on his face was beyond pain, beyond anguish. She had done that to him.

She had one fleeting thought before Stern forced her to turn around, to turn her back on Gabriel. She had not ever seen Gabriel look that way.

Not even when he had been talking to the picture of Julie.

''We're doing something, man. *We are.* We had officers at the scene before you even left it.''

Gabriel looked into Bobby Gandy's tired eyes. Someone—more than one someone—had called 911 on various cell phones. The cops had been peppered by a frenzy of calls. But it had happened a fraction of time too late. By the time the NYPD had gotten to

La Guardia, sirens screaming, Stern, Jr., and Shawna had been gone.

Gabriel moved away from Bobby's desk, feeling like a caged animal. He had gone beyond nausea when he had allowed Stern to take her away. Now his stomach was clamped in a fist of icy iron. His bones were achingly cold. He was sweating.

"You look like hell, my friend," Bobby said. "You need to go somewhere, take a step back from this, calm down."

Gabriel turned on Bobby. *"He's got her."*

"We've got every uniform in the city out there." Bobby sat at his desk, stood, then sat again. He hooked one foot over his thigh and jiggled it.

"What about the park?" Stern hadn't taken her back to his apartment. The cops had already looked there. And they'd found Stern's own telephones tapped to the max, monitoring and tracing every call that came into his residence. It was how he had known where Gabriel and Shawna were calling from. Another angle Gabriel hadn't seen.

Paranoia, Gabriel thought. And utter and complete control over his world. Until he'd gotten distracted by Shawna.

"If he takes her to the park," Bobby said, "then we've got him. We've got men in place."

"It's a lot of ground to cover."

"We have a lot of men. And we're covering every spot he's likely to go."

"That we can think of."

Bobby nodded, conceding that.

"I can't stand here doing nothing!"

Bobby took a mouthful of his own coffee, then he spit it back into the cup, grimacing in disgust. "No offense, pal, but everything you've done so far has more or less ended in disaster.''

He'd done nothing, Gabriel thought. Nothing. And that was going to kill her.

Denial was painful, something thorny pushing up against the inside of his skin. But there was no getting around it. Stern had her. Stern wanted her. And what he might do to her was unimaginable.

Gabriel paced back to Bobby's desk. ''One more time. I want to talk through it all one more time. Everything we know. Maybe there's a clue in there as to where he's taken her.''

Bobby rose again. ''It's senseless. You've already told me everything that happened. But, hey, way to go, figuring out that DNA.'' Bobby gave a short, cracking laugh.

On the desk opposite Bobby's, where Belle had been napping, she shot suddenly to her feet, paws scrambling on papers. She growled. Gabriel looked at her and his blood went cold.

If she hadn't gotten loose from him in the airport parking lot, if she hadn't torn back for the terminal as fast as those stubby little legs had been able to carry her, if Gabriel hadn't wasted precious time pursuing her—wondering even as he did if he was out of his mind—then he would not even have known that Stern had Shawna. He would have been in the car, speeding for their meeting in the city, when Stern caught her. He would have thought Shawna was safe on that plane.

Gabriel's hands shook, his throat hurt, and he thought he was going to vomit.

Bobby came around the desk to clamp a hand on

his shoulder. ''Easy. Hey, man, take it easy. You are falling apart.''

''I've got it together.''

''Like hell. Listen to me. You want some advice? Go home.''

Gabriel's hands fisted unconsciously.

''No, listen,'' Bobby said. ''I have a thought or two here. Stern's got her. But he didn't have her shot at, did he? He didn't try to have *her* killed. Because he obsessed on her. Somewhere along the line his mind got hooked all around her. He wants her home. And that saved your backside, pal. He might have killed you if he hadn't gotten sidetracked with wanting just her. You know, you ought to get down on your knees and thank God she got tangled up in this. It saved your life.''

''Your point?'' Gabriel snarled.

''He's not going to kill her. Not before we can find them. He's got no reason to.''

Gabriel's mind stopped.

''Stern, Jr., has unfinished business with you. If you go somewhere where he can find you, I think you'll hear from him. You could flush him out.''

What had Stern, Jr., said on the phone? We'll make an exchange.

Stern already had what he wanted. For a moment Gabriel's knees went weak. He pulled himself back yet again from the brink of terror.

Stern had what he wanted, but maybe there was something else he wanted more.

Gabriel thought back to one of his first impressions of the killer, standing in Shawna's living room, talking about her roommate. He didn't kill for the pleasure of killing. But he would do it again to save himself. He might do *a lot* to save himself.

And he was essentially a coward.

"What are you going to do?" Bobby asked when Gabriel started for the door. Belle leaped off the desk and bulleted after him.

"I'm going to the television stations. It's time to send a little message to Stern, Jr."

"Chief wants as much of a lid on this—"

"I don't work for Chief anymore."

"Gabe, damn it, come on—"

Gabriel stopped at the door and looked back. "She has one prayer. He's got to feel the net closing in on him." All he had was a hunch, but it—like so much else that had taken place in the last few days—told him that given the opportunity, Stern, Jr., would try to run.

And God bless his warped, wicked soul if he had harmed a hair on Shawna's head first.

Gabriel left the Homicide Bureau with no true plan other than that he had to reach the man, had to get word to him, had to challenge him, give him options, somehow. He took the elevator down and headed for the lot where he had left the rental car. Then he thought about borrowing Bobby's city car instead. It would be identifiable by the cops roaming all over the city right now on a manhunt. And he could park anywhere he had to.

He turned back inside, Belle trotting along at his heels. Went back up in the elevator. Bobby was still at his desk.

"Hey," Bobby said, surprised, hanging up the phone when he saw him. "Change your mind?"

"I want to borrow your unmarked."

"I don't have it. It's in the garage. Something with the radiator. I'm using my truck these days."

The edges of Gabriel's vision went suddenly dark.

Dominos, he thought with strange detachment. *Click,* one falls over. *Bump,* there goes two. And then the whole damned row went down.

Click—red Dodge Ram. He'd known it, hadn't been able to place it. Because, he realized, he'd been so far removed from the fabric of his old life for so long now.

Bump— Hey, way to go, figuring out that DNA. And that nervous laugh afterward.

What had he said? That Stern had obsessed on Shawna? How had he known any of that? Gabriel had never told him that those bullets hadn't seemed to be aimed at Shawna.

Bobby had handed his messages about the time line over to the D.A. He *said* he had—and Gabriel hadn't had a single reason not to believe him. But it wasn't the D.A. who had thought to silence him because he didn't agree with their indictment.

Shawna had been close, very close, but not quite on the mark. The *cops*—at least one cop—had been involved with his car going up.

A cop who had once been his own partner. Gabriel gave a guttural roar and charged Bobby's desk.

He launched himself over the dull gray metal. They crashed backward into the chair. It flew out from beneath them, spinning, tearing across linoleum, until it cracked into the wall. They went down, Gabriel on top. Belle danced around them, yipping furiously.

He wrapped a hand in his friend's collar. "Tell me before I kill you."

Bobby's face was white. "It's not the way you see it."

Gabriel gathered more of his collar, lifted him and cracked his head against the floor. "Don't lie to me anymore!"

"Cool out!" Bobby gripped his fist, trying to loosen it. "I never did anything to hurt you!"

"You blew my car up!"

"You were ten damned yards away at the time!"

The dark at the edges of Gabriel's vision went red.

"Listen!" Bobby shouted. "Just listen to me! I figured it out, even before you did!"

Gabriel tightened his hold.

"I saw that the time of death had to be off, right at the start, even before you came back at me with that. And we had the simple DNA, the Alpha tests, back early. And there were things you didn't know, things I never told you. Damn it, it was going to be my collar! I *had* that bastard! And you weren't a cop anymore! So I didn't share it with you. I didn't share it with anybody! There was nothing you could do, and you were too torn up to be rational at the time, anyway. I figured I'd take care of it. For you. For Julie. And it all went wrong."

Abruptly, without warning, Gabriel let him go. Bobby rubbed his neck, sat up. "I went to Stern, Jr. I was all ready to confront him with the time line and the DNA—try to see if he flinched first."

"What happened?" Deadly calm now, Gabriel realized. That was all that filled him.

"He threatened Kelsey and the kids."

Kelsey? Bobby's *wife?* It wasn't what Gabriel had expected to hear. He'd thought there'd be money involved, some other kind of coercion.

It had been Kelsey, Gabriel thought...and the glory of taking Stern down himself.

"I knew he could do it, even behind bars. Hell, with the scum in the pen, with their connections, Stern's money, she was dead if I took him in. Police protection?" Bobby laughed hoarsely. "We know how that goes. He started showing up when Kelsey would walk the dog at night. She'd tell me she saw him, that he stopped her to say hello. He was playing games with my mind. He warned me. So I backed off that first night, and I stayed back." Bobby stood unsteadily and gave Gabriel a hand up. "All I had to do to keep my family safe was steer things away from Stern, Jr."

"Things?"

"Mostly you."

The red stole further over Gabriel's eyesight.

"Man, look at you. *Look* at you. You came unglued after Julie died. Look at you now that he's taken this woman! You've got to know what it is to protect the people you love! Man, it's my *family*."

"Oh, I know."

"Damn it, those bullets never came near you! I gave the guys the word to scare you, not take you! I made damned sure you were one step clear all along!"

"You should have told me. You should have let me in at the beginning. Between the two of us, we would have had him by now." And Shawna would be safe in Philadelphia.

Calmly, deliberately, Gabriel drew back his fist and smashed it into his friend's jaw.

As Bobby slid down the wall again, spitting blood, Gabriel reached down and took his revolver. "I might need this. Go ahead, *buddy*. Report me."

Chapter 16

Stern, Jr., had deposited her on the sofa.

Shawna wasn't hurt. Yet. The cut on her neck had to have been superficial, because she was reasonably sure that it had stopped bleeding. But she was uncomfortable. Stern had bound her wrists and ankles with duct tape that he'd found in the kitchen. There was no need to paste a piece across her mouth. She could scream her throat raw, and no one would hear her, not in Julie's little mountain home.

She focused on him, trying to keep her eyes on him and off the room. Because it was like some kind of twisted nightmare to notice the bowl of soup she'd put on the floor for Belle earlier, their bags still off in the corner of the sitting room, the table where she and Gabriel had fallen into each other, making love as though they might have a future.

He would never think to look for them here. Not

unless or until he had figured out the connection between Stern and Julie.

She bit down hard on her lip to keep from crying out with the hopelessness that clawed up in her throat, then something inside her rallied. She thought of the last she had seen of Gabriel's face. He loved her. Maybe he didn't even know it yet, but she was sure. They only had a chance of exploring that if she could get off this mountain alive.

She'd done everything she could to save him. She was damned if she was going to die now.

She watched Stern move back and forth, past the table, into the kitchen, then he returned. Occasionally he scrubbed a hand over his mouth. His hand trembled when he did it. And then something amazing struck her, something that she hadn't yet figured out.

"You're *scared*."

Stern, Jr., looked at her sharply. "Don't be an idiot, darling. It's beneath you."

She shifted her weight. Her left arm ached from being twisted unnaturally behind her. He started to come toward her. Shawna worked up a smile and went still again. "I'm a lawyer, you know. Just about, anyway."

She'd played the wrong hand. His expression went deadly. "It's people like you who'd want to hang me."

"No. I want to help you."

She couldn't look at his hands. If she looked at his hands, if she thought of what they had done to Julie, she would go crazy.

"If they take me in, it's over," he said almost conversationally. "They want the death penalty for my father."

"But your father's already in jail. You could still get away."

Nothing, no response. Taking it as a good sign, she pushed on. "It's going to take them a while to get all the paperwork in order on you. They can't just take you. They'll need a warrant." It wasn't entirely true, but she gambled that he didn't know that. "They'll have to find a cooperative judge. It'll take a little time because they already have your father in custody, and all they really have on you is your strange behavior this morning."

He was watching her intently. She had him.

"Of course, if Gabriel talks, then it is over."

Her heart thudded sickly with the risk she was taking. But her mind was all she'd ever had.

She'd been an ugly duckling in high school, a bookworm. Through college, she'd been too driven to care. In law school, toward the end, she'd bored nearly every man she'd gone out with. And she had been oh, so bored with them.

She had *never* felt, never cared, never been a part of anything important, until Gabriel. Until this. Oh, she loved him.

Stern, Jr., came to her. He reached a hand out to her. Shawna's muscles tightened in on themselves and recoiled from him of their own volition. She held her bland smile, but everything inside her screamed.

"You are incredible," he murmured. "I knew it from the first moment you lured Marsden out of that apartment."

"I didn't—"

"I knew you had to be special. I was going to kill you, you know. After I saw you, after I had you, because then you'd know who I was. And I was going to try to keep my life, just go on. But this is better. We can run away together.

Her stomach rolled over. "I'll help you get away," she agreed carefully.

He pulled his hand back from her cheek. Shawna breathed again.

"You're not safe here," she pressed on. "All you can do is leave the country before the D.A.'s office gets their act together. You know that. You just said it. You can't have your old life back. Because I've been with Gabriel for days now, and I know that he knows everything. And he won't just go away, especially now that you've got me. He'll do something with the information. So you've got to get away fast."

She saw in his insane eyes that he wanted to believe her.

She would have waved a hand if one had been free. Instead, she shrugged the one shoulder that could still barely move. "Of course, maybe there's…I don't know, some mitigating circumstance. Something that would make them go easy on you."

"Of course, there is," Stern said irritably. "I loved her."

Shawna went with her gut, with her heart. "You were so much alike. But she wouldn't leave Gabriel."

Stern's face turned ugly. "She said he'd done nothing to deserve it."

Shawna felt tears come to her eyes. She fought them off for the hundredth time.

"She wanted to stop it! Stop us! She called it an attack of conscience! It was over!"

"Not for you."

"Never for me."

Love, she thought weakly, was the most powerful

impetus known to man. Not even Julie would betray Gabriel, not in the end. For his sake, Shawna wanted desperately to believe that it was because Julie had loved him once.

"You came here with her." She'd already noticed the way Stern moved about the place, knowing his way. And then there was the matter of all the food Julie had laid in. More than for a passing visit. "I'm sorry."

And then he was weeping. Shawna watched, horrified.

"I *loved* her," he said again.

"I know."

"We were supposed to go to France together. She said we should buy separate tickets so Marsden would never catch on. We were going to stay there forever. Fine wine. Good food. We'd learn a new language and make love in Paris in the springtime."

Yes, she thought now, seeing.

"But she never really bought the ticket. She came to the airport. No luggage. Nothing. Said it was off. *We* were off."

"You never got on that plane." Another shot in the dark. This time she was wrong.

"I went. I turned right around and came back again. I never even left the airport."

The last piece of the puzzle, Shawna thought. He *had* been on that plane, in that seat. But he'd come straight home again. Her heart squeezed, stealing breath. Would Gabriel have ever figured that out?

"I went to Talia as soon as I got back," Stern said. "Talia would understand. But she laughed at me for taking Julie seriously. She said Julie didn't know what she wanted. I should never have believed anything she said, and I was a fool if I had. Then Julie arrived.''

Shawna could only imagine the hell that had unfolded then.

''She said she wasn't going to change her mind. She said things. That he was better than I was. And I got angry.''

''You are in so much danger,'' she breathed. ''He's still out there. And my God, the whole city has to be looking for you. You're probably on TV right now. You'll be in every news broadcast, just for taking me the way you did. And if Gabriel talks about how you killed Julie, too—''

Stern, Jr.'s, eyes went a little wild. *Hunted.* He went to the television in the large living area. Shawna squeezed her eyes shut. And she prayed with all her faith, all her belief, to every idea that had carried her through twenty-seven years. Because if there was *any* angel, anywhere, involved in all this, then oh, how she needed *something* regarding John Thomas Stern, Jr., to be on that television now.

Stern turned it on. And there was Gabriel.

Shawna cried out in shock, yet oddly unsurprised. Her heart flooded at the sight of his face.

''Shut *up!*'' Stern shouted.

Shawna bit down on her lip hard.

''—here's the deal,'' Gabriel said from the screen. ''I just want her back.''

What was he doing? Then, in a heartbeat, Shawna understood. She looked quickly at Stern. He was watching the television, mesmerized.

''Bring her to the place we were going to meet earlier. In two hours. If she's there, you can walk away from this. If not, I'll bring in every law enforce-

ment agency I ever had contact with and we'll find
you. You'll wish to God you'd gone when you had
the chance." Gabriel looked dead into the camera.
"It's your call. Two hours."

It was a message only she and Stern would understand. Come back, and if the cops figured a connection between what had happened to Shawna and what
had happened to Julie, it would not come from Gabriel. He wasn't going to talk.

Everything went to jelly inside her. No.

She knew what vengeance meant to Gabriel. She
knew what Stern, Jr., had done to him. For a year
now, Gabriel had lived to see this man pay for his
crimes.

It was a bluff. Except…she saw his face again
when Stern had taken her away.

She found her voice. "What are you going to do?"

Stern, Jr., was pacing now, agitated. "*Fool.* What
a fool he must think I am. If we go to the theater,
there will be cops waiting."

"No. Maybe not. He was making you a promise."

"If they heard what he said, they'll go there, anyway."

"No. Not if he hasn't told them you were going to
meet him this morning at the theater. How would they
know where to go?"

But Stern was fretting. "Why would he do that?
Why would he let me go?"

To get me back. She felt weak with it. "He loves
me."

Stern came to her, pulled her to her feet. Her heart
thudded.

"We'll go to the theater," he agreed. "Yes, I think
we'll do that. It could work if we get there first, before

he does. In and out. Fast. Then we'll get out of the country. Do you have a passport?''

"Uh...no." Something like silken spider webs was filling her mind. A passport? She wouldn't need a passport if he was going to leave her at the theater and run.

"That's a problem. But if we can get out of New York, we can work on it."

He steered her toward the door. He laughed, shrilly, a sound that teetered on the edge of insanity then cracked and plunged over. "But first we've got to kill Marsden. He has been such a nuisance, darling, such a thorn in my side from the start. You know he deserves it."

Adrenaline burned in his blood. Fear made his muscles feel like water. One chance, Gabriel thought as the cab drew up on Forty-third and Broadway.

"Place is closed up tight," said the driver, looking at the theater.

"Yeah. Look, I need you to sit here for a while."

"Gonna cost you."

"I don't care."

Gabriel left the dog curled on the back seat. Her head popped up when he got out of the car, and she wore an odd expression that he couldn't read. Knowing? Pitying? If she was psychic, if she could see into the future, Gabriel didn't want to know about it.

He went around to the back of the theater. His hands weren't quite steady as he lifted Bobby's gun and cracked the butt down on the first of the locks on the theater's back door. The clasp sprung and he went to work on the others. Finally, he shoved the gun down inside his belt and went inside.

For a moment he only stood inside the door, his eyes adjusting to the lack of light. The place had been closed for six months. Gabriel stepped around forgotten props in the storage area, over a flounced dress that somehow had gotten strewn on the floor of the hallway.

His heart thundered.

He reached the stage area from the rear and stepped out into a sensation of cavernous darkness. He went to front and center stage and sat down.

He did not know how much time passed. He lost his sense of it as memories flicked through his mind—an image of Shawna popping that stale chip into her mouth, her eyes as she had looked out at the city lights. Julie had craved, he thought. Shawna had asked for so little.

Would Stern bring her? Had the man even seen the news? If he had, Gabriel knew his message would have been like a gauntlet thrown down. If he'd seen it, he would come.

Then Stern's voice sneered through a microphone somewhere as though in answer to Gabriel's prayers.

"Always in the spotlight, front and center, thinking you're the best."

Gabriel's pulse ricocheted, then his heart seemed to literally stop as a spotlight snapped on, blinding him.

One chance. There was no room for emotion, for reaction, for feeling. He knew that if he got up and tried to move, Stern would only follow him with the spotlight. He would achieve nothing but to give Stern the satisfaction.

So he continued to sit. One bullet could take him out. He would never even feel it.

He spoke quietly. "You can get away if you leave the country now."

"Don't take me for a fool!" Anger hummed beneath Stern's voice, a frenzied peevishness. "You're not going to keep quiet! Why would you?"

Where was Shawna?

"They don't have enough on you yet to bring you in. But they're working on it. You could still go now. Just leave me with Shawna."

"No offense, Mr. Marsden, but I don't believe you. You could have police surrounding this place at any time." He paused. "Let me explain to you how this is going to work. You are removed. Then, as you said, I flee safely. The lovely Shawnalee and I will fly off together, perhaps to Europe. I win. This time, I get the lady. But I can't leave you dangling here, ready to talk, so they can just find me and drag me home again. And, of course, we don't have much time."

As plans went, Gabriel thought, it was a good one. Stern held all the cards.

He'd gotten him here. His bluff had worked this far. But, in the end, he had nothing Stern either wanted or needed, nothing to barter.

Yes, Gabriel thought, one of them certainly was going to have to die.

Bobby's gun felt heavy, its metal hot against his waist. It was nearly at his back, and he did not know if Stern had yet noticed it. But with the spotlight on him, he couldn't reach for it. By the time he got his hand on it, if Stern was armed, he was dead.

Besides, the light was blinding him. He'd be shooting into silver-white light. The microphone gave him no angle on Stern's voice. He did not know where he

was. At the other end of the light? Possibly. But he
might have aimed the thing and moved on.

He had to take a chance on getting out off the stage.
Ahead of him, tiers of seating stretched out. The
lights, of course, could fan the audience, as well. But
there, at least, Stern might lose him. He had a better
chance of hiding there than here on this wide-open
stage.

Hold on, lady. I'll find you.

Braced for tearing pain, for the intrusion of metal
into his body, Gabriel moved suddenly and without
warning, diving off the stage and rolling into the seating.

In the cab outside, Belle snapped awake from her
doze. A growl rumbled in her throat and she stood,
yipping, then she hurled herself at the window.

The driver had been in his own state of semicon-
sciousness, nodding off while he waited. He jerked
awake and looked into the back seat.

"Hey, hey! What do you think you're doing
there?"

Belle snapped and bit at the armrest, going for the
handle.

"Knock that off! You tear that up on my time, I
gotta pay for it!"

The dog seemed oblivious to his protests. Why the
hell had he allowed an animal in the car in the first
place?

The driver twisted in his seat and started to reach
for her. But man, he did not like dogs. And with the
frenzy this one was in he was sure as hell she would
bite him.

No fare was worth this. Her teeth and claws were already doing damage to the car.

Damned if he was waiting around for that guy any longer, he thought. He was moonlighting to begin with, putting in his second eight-hour shift of the day. What could the cab company do, fire him for losing a man and a dog? Stranger things happened all the time.

The driver craned over the seat, got past the mutt to the doorhandle, and threw the door open fast. The dog bulleted out of the car.

''Good riddance,'' the driver grumbled. Then he put the car in drive and coasted off.

This time Stern had taped her mouth. And her wrists and ankles were still bound.

In one of the dressing rooms, straining to hear something, *anything,* Shawna stood carefully from the chair Stern had left her in. She struggled for balance. She tried to hop toward the door and lost the battle. She went down hard with a muffled cry.

Well, she thought desperately, nobody said she had to walk. She rocked a bit to gather momentum, then she rolled toward the door.

She almost wept with relief when she saw that Stern hadn't closed it completely. She used her forehead and her shoulder to nudge it open wider. And then she froze.

Barking? Belle? Gabriel had brought Belle into the theater for this showdown?

Something hysterical hit her. She giggled helplessly. And then the dog was there, licking her face, and the bitter tears her laughter gave way to.

Belle. Incredibly, the dog began nipping at the tape

at her mouth. Pulling it off. Shawna felt one quick, disbelieving kick of her heart as the tape came free with a painful tug, Belle's little teeth secure on the end of it. But then, she realized, she was not particularly surprised at all.

"Good girl," she whispered when she could talk. "Good, good dog. My hands, baby, can you do my hands? It's just tape."

Belle trotted around behind her and gnawed obediently.

The second hand on her watch seemed to boom. Her heart clamored right along with it. It was so quiet out there. What was happening? What were they doing? She could not even hear voices.

Then she did hear something—Stern's crazed giggle. And the cracking sound of wood splintering, giving way. Shouts, sounding muffled. And something crashing.

Belle chewed some slack in the tape. Shawna yanked her hands hard and broke free the rest of the way. Her skin felt as though it was tearing away with the tape.

She groped with the tape at her ankles, adhered to her jeans.

She got it off, pushed to her feet and ran.

She headed toward the front of the theater where the sounds were coming from. Her own voice was a series of short little cries and prayers.

She came up from the wing, racing out onto the stage. And she saw them. A spotlight was skewed oddly, throwing a beam of light against a wall. But it spilled thin light over the seating, as well, and that was where she found them.

Fighting. Crashing over the row of one line of seats

onto another. Briefly into the glare of the spotlight, then out again into relative darkness. Shawna saw the glint of a knife in Stern's hand in a moment of light, and she screamed.

For one frozen moment, both men stopped to look her way. Shawna leaped off the stage, stumbling a little, then she raced up the nearest aisle toward them.

"Get back!" Gabriel's voice. No, she wouldn't listen to him this time, either.

Shawna climbed up onto a seat, clambered over it onto the next. What could she do? Gabriel had Stern's knife hand in one fist, holding it at bay. His other came back, then smashed down. Blood flew. Shawna cried out again. They rolled. Stern's hand was white-knuckled and straining around the knife.

And then they rolled half under the seats. There was a different kind of clatter. Something dull. A thud. They grappled further under the seat and Shawna saw a gun on the floor behind them.

Stern kicked it in his struggles and it skidded halfway down the aisle, toward her. Shawna jumped down from the seat and grabbed it in both hands. She climbed up onto the chair again.

"Stop!" She cocked the revolver. The click echoed in a fresh wave of brief, stunned quiet.

Gabriel looked up, and in that moment Stern wrenched his knife hand from his grip. He drew back—and Shawna fired.

She had never been a good shot. Her brothers had hunted back in Kansas—she knew shotguns, not revolvers. The bullet burned a hole through red upholstery eight inches above Stern's shoulder.

Damn it! She realized in that moment that she was ready to kill. If it meant Gabriel's life, she would do it. She cocked the gun again, shaking. She had to stop shaking.

But the shock of the fire cost Stern, Jr., a moment's hesitation. And in that moment Gabriel brought his fist down again hard.

Shawna cried out, softly this time, and looked away. There was a groan, more thuds of flesh against flesh. She had to see. She glanced back just as Stern's hand loosened.

The knife fell from it. Shawna jumped down from the seat again and grabbed it just as it clattered to the wood.

Stern's eyes had rolled back in his head. He wasn't moving. And Shawna felt black beginning to creep over her own vision.

Not again.

Gabriel got to his feet and caught her before she went down.

"I...I...I..." she began.

"It's all right." His voice was soothing, crooning. "Here. Give it here. Let it go."

He pried the revolver from one hand, then the knife from the other. Back in the aisle, Belle barked, then began running toward the stage again.

Gabriel held her, the scent of sunflowers winding through his senses. He felt the warmth of her, the life beating in her heart against his own. She dug her fingers into his shirt and held on.

Alive, he thought. She'd come out of nowhere, and she'd saved his life...and his soul.

Chapter 17

"That is so incredible!" Katie cried. "Then what happened?"

Shawna scraped her hair back with a headband and leaned closer to the bedroom mirror without answering. How was it, she wondered helplessly, that she could look exactly as she had less than a week ago? She should be changed somehow. She should be different.

But none of the scars seemed to show.

She had been home for two days, and even the purple smudges were gone from beneath her eyes. She'd been caught up in a whirlwind of newspaper interviews, and the NYPD had sent detectives to talk to her. This was the first opportunity she'd had to catch up with Katie.

"Then," she murmured finally, "we went outside to a phone booth and called the cops."

"You just left Stern in the theater?"

"Well, we had to. And he wasn't going any-where." But they'd gone back inside to make sure, to stand guard over the man, until the police had ar-rived.

That was when she'd told him what she'd learned at the cabin.

He hadn't guessed of Julie's infidelity. He'd said he hadn't known. Of course, they'd both known there was *some* relationship between Stern and Julie. But only Shawna had realized that the rage, the passion, with which he had slaughtered her said so much more. People killed like that when love had gone wrong.

Maybe Gabriel had chosen *not* to see. Because what she had told him in the theater had stunned him. And then she'd lost him, as she had feared from the first that she would.

When it was all over at the theater, he'd said that he would call her. But his gaze had been pointed be-yond her shoulder at the time, and then he'd taken her back to the airport. Two days had gone by now without a word from him.

A gentle letdown, she thought. The very worst kind.

"I still can't believe that *you* were the unidentified female companion," Katie said, and Shawna jolted back to the present.

She winced. In the end, that just about described the size of the impact she'd had on Gabriel's life, after all. For a moment her heart felt as if it would seize.

"And I never put it together with your out-of-the-blue trip to Kansas," Katie rattled on. "I didn't rec-ognize Gabriel Marsden from the pictures they flashed on television as that man we saw on the corner."

"Well, the last year's been hard on him. He's changed some."

"Gabriel Marsden. This is unreal."

Shawna stepped away from the mirror. She was as ready as she was ever going to be, she supposed.

She was taking the bar exam in an hour.

And that, she thought, was the only real meaning she could find in anything that had happened to them. Fate had tossed her into Gabriel's path so justice could be served. She had been a catalyst and nothing more, carrying the money and the dog into his life. Gabriel had needed that old woman's money, and Belle had saved his life. And, of course, her own.

Now a guilty man was in jail, and an innocent man had gone free. Her reward—such as it was—was a realized sense of purpose. In its convoluted, bizarre way, fate had shown her her path.

Shawna took a breath and headed for the door.

"You know, I'm not sure you should be doing this today," Kate said from behind her, scrambling off the bed to follow her into the living room.

"They were kind enough to give me a makeup day. I didn't want to drag it out too long. Don't worry. I'll pass."

"But, you know, there are things like posttraumatic stress syndrome and whatnot," Katie insisted. "You should probably take it easy for another couple of days."

"I'm fine." She felt broken.

"Shawna, you've been making national headlines for days now. I don't think the bar would feel any qualm about giving you some more time to, you know, come to terms with all this and prepare for the test."

"I studied plenty before I was chased off by a murderer. Besides, I meet with the Public Defender's Office tomorrow. I want to wrap all this up and get on with my life."

The public defender was champing at the bit to hire her. The interview was more or less a formality. She'd begin working there on Monday as a paralegal until her exam results came through.

She'd spend the rest of her life saving others who had been falsely accused. It would be enough. She'd probably never get that penthouse apartment on a P.D.'s salary. But for one glimmering priceless moment, she'd had her city lights.

Shawna beat back tears and reached for the doorknob. As soon as she touched it, a knock sounded on the other side. Startled, she jumped back and cried out.

"See?" Katie demanded. "That's exactly what I'm talking about. You're still spooked."

"Paranoia is a learned response." Her heart squeezed again. Gabriel's words.

She opened the door. A cop waited on the other side. She scowled at him for a moment before she recognized him. It was the officer from her mugging.

"Ms. Collins?"

She opened her mouth and closed it again. Her heart plunged down to her toes.

"I can get it back for her," she blurted. "You found the old woman, right? She wants her box back? I can take care of it." If nothing else, she knew Gabriel would replace the money. He always did the right thing. He'd keep his word. "But—oh, God— I'll have to buy her a new Chihuahua. She saved me, and I saved Gabriel, but then she was just—gone."

The cop looked bemused. "Uh, well, I don't think you have to worry about returning anything. I just stopped by to let you know that we found the woman. You know, after you gave me your statement that day, I kept a watch out for her around that corner. But it was actually a fluke that I found her. She was...ah, unclaimed at the hospital."

Shawna narrowed her eyes at him warily. "Unclaimed...how?"

"She must have gone there right after she dumped all that stuff on you. She died there within the day. Cancer."

Shawna pressed a hand to her mouth.

"She had no kin to bury her, and that always causes some paperwork for the city. I came across it, and...well, the housecoat she showed up at the hospital in matches your description."

Shawna had a horrible thought. "I don't have to identify her, do I?" She'd looked at enough pictures of bodies this week to last her a lifetime.

The cop shook his head quickly. "No. But she had a few things in her pockets, and...I don't know, she seemed to want you to have those other things, so I...uh, brought these, too." He looked embarrassed. "I thought you might be...interested in them."

For the first time in days Shawna felt something other than pain in her heart. "That's kind of you."

He took a pathetically small envelope from his pocket. "Here you go."

When he was gone, Shawna slit it and opened it. There was some battered, beaten ID. She could barely make out the name. She squinted, held it closer.

Jeannine Stern. Coincidence? There was no such thing. Shawna sucked in her breath.

There was a small silver locket on a delicate chain.
And an old photo of what she could only assume was
of a man she had loved, maybe married. She unfolded
a worn piece of paper. A love letter. His name had
been Harry.

Shawna smiled sadly. Katie took the locket and
popped it open. Then her jaw fell. "Oh, my God,
Shawna. No wonder she gave you that money."

Shawna took the locket back and peered at the
small gray photograph. A face smiled back at her, a
young woman who might well have been her sister.
She felt her skin pull into gooseflesh.

"See, there wasn't anything fateful or mystical
about it at all," Katie went on, ever practical. "You
just reminded her of someone. I bet that was probably
her daughter. That's why she stopped you. That's why
she chose you."

Shawna put the locket in her pocket. It was probably as simple as that, she thought. The most convoluted things usually were.

But somehow, in her heart, she didn't believe it.

A hundred miles away Gabriel dug the heels of his
hands into his tired eyes. And he saw her again.

Why couldn't he get her out of his mind?

He sat back from his desk. He stared at the dull
words on his computer screen. He had made up his
mind to do it this way. Neatly and in the order in
which he had first intended. But Shawna wouldn't go
away and leave him alone.

Why didn't that surprise him?

He sat forward again. To write of Julie. That was
his plan now. Not murder articles full of insight for
Reynold, but a book. Maybe someday he would sell

it. More likely, when it was finished, he would stick it into a drawer.

He was doing what he had started doing eleven months ago. He was going through it all moment by moment, memory by memory, so that he could put Julie—and her death—behind him. Until then, he knew he had nothing to give Shawna at all.

At least nothing that a woman like her, with her hope and her brightness, deserved.

He'd been writing more or less constantly for two days now, since he had come home. There'd been little in the way of sleep, less in the way of food. Too much like before when he hadn't had the answers and had been driven to learn more.

The problem, of course, was that he could not see Julie anymore. The images he created of her seemed flat. He couldn't capture her, what she had been or how she had betrayed him.

He wondered again, if she had lived, if she had come home that night, would she ever have told him of her infidelity? He knew somewhere in his soul that she probably would have. In a moment of anger she would have spat it at him, her claws bared for a good fight.

Guilt had been his intimate friend for nearly a year now—and in that theater, in a few short sentences, when Shawna had told him the truth, it had grown. Fresh life had been breathed into it until it had become a gnarly monster. Now he knew how *literally* he had caused Julie's death. Not by failing to go out with her that night. Instead his indifference had driven her straight into the arms of a madman.

The phone rang, and Gabriel jolted. The images in

his mind shredded, fell apart. Would she call him? Of course she would. She never gave up.

He reached across the desk and grabbed the phone. "Hello?"

"What you need to do is to stop brooding, get out of that apartment and have a good, stiff drink," came Reynold's voice. "I can meet you in ten minutes."

Gabriel thought about it. He was afraid that if he drank, he'd come undone. All the careful control he'd managed to muster since leaving that theater would unwind.

At his silence Reynold went on. "Well then, maybe a cup of coffee and the chance to talk about it. This isn't healthy, Gabe."

"I'm not brooding. I'm writing about it," Gabriel said finally.

Reynold's response was quick and plain. "Why?"

Gabriel stared at the computer screen. To purge, he answered silently, to make sense of it all, to box it all up neatly and set it aside so he could go on without the baggage. As always, he was organized. He had his priorities.

"Same reason as before."

"So you can spend another year of your life beating yourself up over it?" Reynold scoffed. "Gabe, I'm a patient man. But watching you do this is pushing me to the wall."

Gabriel felt anger stir—good, clean, healthy anger. "If you've got something to say, Reynold, then say it."

"Sure. I was just waiting for the invitation. You've been torturing yourself over this since the night Julie died. Punishing yourself. Locking yourself in dark rooms and doing penance because you failed at something. Whoa, pal, you think you're above the rest of us?" He paused. "By the way, whatever happened to your unidentified female companion?"

Gabriel snarled. "Shawna. Shawnalee Collins. You know her name." And never once had Reynold released it to the press. They'd only IDed her after it was all over.

America knew her name now. Her face and everything else about her had been all over the news since this had ended. But not in any interview he'd seen since then had she spoken a single word about fate or karma.

That, more than anything else, scared the hell out of him. The light had gone out of her. Gabriel was organized, he was doing this right, waiting until he had a free heart to give her, if she even wanted it. But she didn't seem to *believe* anymore.

Gabriel hung up without saying another word. Reynold called right back again.

"Gabe, it's *over*. Let it go."

And then Reynold hung up. Gabriel grimaced. Reynold always did have to have the last word.

But as far as friends went, he, at least, was a true one. Gabriel had told him of the suspicions that had ridden him for days regarding his involvement. Sure you thought that, Reynold had said. I would have thought I did it, too. Hell, you only had two choices.

He still could not quite think about the friend who had failed him.

Gabriel turned back to the computer screen. He wrote some, and he wondered again what had happened to that nasty little dog.

And then something eerie came over him. Something that had him moving uncomfortably in his chair.

Shawna's voice rang in his head again. *I thought you were some kind of angel.*

That dog had just plain *disappeared.* She'd been no more than five steps ahead of them when they'd left that theater the first time. They'd gone out the rear door, had looked left, had looked right, and Belle had been gone.

After saving their lives, she'd just...vanished.

For the first time in days Gabriel heard himself laugh aloud. *That* would make an interesting book, he thought. That growling, pugnacious little beast proving to be an angel? He'd always suspected God had a sense of humor.

Thinking of the dog made him remember that he owed that old lady the balance of fifteen thousand dollars. There were strings here left untied, he thought. And hadn't he always hated those?

Strings should always be tied first. Then the healing could begin.

The words weren't coming. For a year he had dreamed of coming back to this, and now the halls of his apartment echoed and the rooms were cold. The only life on the computer screen was born of Shawna. So many of the ultimate answers had come through her insights. It was impossible to remove her from the story. She peppered the pages. The magic spell of her wound through every scene.

Gabriel stood. He didn't bother with a coat this time. Sometime during the last week, spring had arrived at last. He left the apartment and locked up behind himself—one lock on this door. The corridor was well lit. No smells and no canned laughter. Just cushioned quiet.

He stood listening to it for a moment, then he went

back inside and took the wedding ring off his right hand. He'd come home, he thought, but there had been nothing here to come back to, after all. He wondered if there was anything left to go to, or if he had lost it all.

Shawna thought the test had gone well. She just had that kind of brain. When something got in there, some snippet of information, it rarely left again. Sometimes she just had to sift through everything else that was stashed in there in order to find what she wanted.

There was no doubt in her mind that she had passed the bar exam.

She left the building, stepping into sunlight that hurt her eyes for a moment. And then she saw Gabriel.

Her heart kicked. He started across the street toward her.

Shawna stopped halfway down the steps of the old, brick building, squinting as her eyes adjusted to the light. Her heart split in two. Part of her wanted to run to him. The other part wanted to run *from* him. But when had she ever been a coward?

Shawna went down the rest of the steps. She stopped in front of him. "Lose something?"

My heart. My mind. "Yeah. But your roommate told me where to find it."

Her heart rolled over.

She would *not* hope again, couldn't bear to believe again. But oh, the loss of hope was the most painful loss of all. She felt her eyes tear.

Gabriel floundered when she didn't answer. Those eyes...so dark, so watchful. Shining now. Waiting.

For the second time since he'd known her, Gabriel
opened his mouth and something he had not planned
to say came out.

"I think I still owe you fifteen thousand dollars."

The look that came over her face—stricken, then
too calm and accepting—made him hate himself. But
her response left him too surprised to react.

"No, you don't, Gabriel." She stepped past him.
"The old lady died."

"The old woman *died?*"

She looked back over her shoulder at him warily.
She said nothing. *That,* Gabriel thought, was unlike
her. It was another bad sign.

He'd been shocked and shattered, he thought, by
what she had told him about Julie. He'd felt wounded
and stupid and blind. But he already knew that the
worst thing he could do to her was shut her out, and
he had done that. When he was hurting the most, he
had pushed her away.

For the *third* time since he had known her, he
opened his mouth and surprised himself. "You know,
maybe *she* was our angel. It was either her, or it was
her dog."

"You don't believe that."

And then, as he watched, wishing desperately that
he wasn't seeing what he was seeing, her tears began
to spill over.

"No," he said quickly. "No, don't do that. Don't
cry."

She swiped at her eyes. "Posttraumatic stress syndrome."

"Well, you've earned it—but, no, Shawna, please.
Don't." And then she was in his arms.

She'd done it before, and he was never quite prepared for it. She came at him fast, hard, without warning, but this time there was nothing behind him. He took a step back, then he held her, held on.

This time she didn't kiss him. She made a fist and brought it against his chest. "I fell in love with you!" There, she thought, it was out and her pride could be damned.

Temper again, he thought, flaring there in her eyes, dark fire.

Then she reared back. "No, no. I'm not asking you to want me. I'm not insisting this time. I *won't*. But you...you can't just come here like this, just stroll back into my life and...and talk about the things that happened to us like you were discussing some quirky weather. Don't you dare make fun of what I believe!"

He was reeling. But he had never done that. Never.

"If it meant nothing to you, you should just leave!" But some of the heat in her eyes was banking, some of the fury was unraveling. Her eyes changed, clouding. She looked hurt and confused.

"I'm sorry." Inane words, he thought, stupid words, and *still* not what he wanted to say. "I was writing about it. I thought I still needed to write about it. I couldn't do that with you distracting me, so I sent you away."

"You should have just said so! I would have been quiet. I wouldn't have gotten in the way."

Gabriel laughed hoarsely. "Right."

He paused, and then finally the right words came. "You were there, anyway. All through it."

She looked up at him again, her eyes still watery. But she went still.

"You brought the answers."

"We did that together."

"No," he said, "no. The big ones. Things like—
you humbled me."

She pulled away from him. He was losing her.

"You wouldn't let me retreat," he said quickly.
"You wouldn't let me keep burrowing."

"You were embroiled in it. That was only natural."

Did she *always* look at the bright side, the kind
side, the forgiving side? "I'm talking about my *life,*
Shawna. All my life! You took the way I was away
from me."

Her eyes widened. And then, finally, he saw there
what he needed to see. Hope.

"You changed everything. I knew you would. But
I didn't know you'd change *me.* Shawna, marry me."

"What?"

"You heard me. I've come to my senses. Look,
don't say anything just yet. Forget I even asked it. I
mean, we've known each other a week. I'm aware of
that. And God knows it hasn't been a normal week.
But let's see what we've got between us without
blood and death and murder. Let's—"

And then she laughed, the sound that he'd finally
understood was just as important as his great pursuit
of vengeance. "Gabriel, you're babbling."

She was right. He was. But then she sobered.

"I can't be Julie."

He watched her, dumbfounded. "No." Thank God.

"I'll never really be what you want."

"You're *everything* I want."

But she shook her head. "I saw you in the garden
room. Talking to her picture. I can't share you with
her, Gabriel." She drew herself up. "I don't want

to." Her voice cracked. "I don't ever want to be second best, a substitute."

And then, clearly, he understood. The last pieces came together. Why she had run that day into the woods, and the danger be damned. Why she hadn't talked to him.

"I was saying goodbye to her. I was going to chuck the whole hunt for her killer and take you to Bora Bora."

She blinked. "Where?"

"Somewhere far away and very cheap. We had a money problem at the time."

Her eyes widened. "Why didn't you just say so?"

"I think the bullets screwed up my train of thought."

She stared at him a moment, then her gaze dropped to his right hand. The ring was gone. She kissed him hard. "Yes!"

"Yes," he murmured.

"I'll marry you," she said against his mouth, then she drew back. "Of course I will. I've figured it all out. Just now. Just this instant."

"What?"

"All the reasons fate threw me in your path. Part of it was justice. You know, that it wasn't going to happen without you and me believing that the truth was worth something."

She had thought the truth was worth something. He'd been fired by shame and rage. But he wouldn't argue with her.

"And that reminded me that law *is* justice, all those shady tax loopholes and personal-injury suits aside. Maybe those things aren't virtuous, but justice still is.

Justice remains. So I'm going to join the Public Defender's Office.''

Gabriel felt some of the air go out of him. He'd been prepared for some serendipitous explanation of what they meant to each other's lives. Instead, he got…justice.

"Okay."

"Then there's the last reason."

"Hmm?"

"We balance each other."

Shawna thought of what Katie had said earlier. Nothing mystical about this? The woman was dead and the dog had disappeared into thin air. But together, they had saved her and Gabriel.

"Lady, I love you."

Shawna smiled and kissed him again. She would never believe it had been anything other than magic.

* * * * *

If you enjoyed what you just read,
then we've got an offer you can't resist!

Take 2 bestselling love stories FREE!

Plus get a FREE surprise gift!

Clip this page and mail it to Silhouette Reader Service™

IN U.S.A.	IN CANADA
3010 Walden Ave.	P.O. Box 609
P.O. Box 1867	Fort Erie, Ontario
Buffalo, N.Y. 14240-1867	L2A 5X3

YES! Please send me 2 free Silhouette Intimate Moments® novels and my free surprise gift. Then send me 6 brand-new novels every month, which I will receive months before they're available in stores. In the U.S.A., bill me at the bargain price of $3.57 plus 25¢ delivery per book and applicable sales tax, if any*. In Canada, bill me at the bargain price of $3.96 plus 25¢ delivery per book and applicable taxes**. That's the complete price and a savings of over 10% off the cover prices—what a great deal! I understand that accepting the 2 free books and gift places me under no obligation ever to buy any books. I can always return a shipment and cancel at any time. Even if I never buy another book from Silhouette, the 2 free books and gift are mine to keep forever. So why not take us up on our invitation. You'll be glad you did!

245 SEN CNFF
345 SEN CNFG

Name	(PLEASE PRINT)	
Address	Apt.#	
City	State/Prov.	Zip/Postal Code

* Terms and prices subject to change without notice. Sales tax applicable in N.Y.
** Canadian residents will be charged applicable provincial taxes and GST.
   All orders subject to approval. Offer limited to one per household.
   ® are registered trademarks of Harlequin Enterprises Limited.

INMOM99   ©1998 Harlequin Enterprises Limited

Don't miss Silhouette's newest cross-line promotion,

Four royal sisters find their own Prince Charmings as they embark on separate journeys to find their missing brother, the Crown Prince!

Royally Wed

The search begins in October 1999 and continues through February 2000:

On sale October 1999: **A ROYAL BABY ON THE WAY** by award-winning author **Susan Mallery** (Special Edition)

On sale November 1999: **UNDERCOVER PRINCESS** by bestselling author **Suzanne Brockmann** (Intimate Moments)

On sale December 1999: **THE PRINCESS'S WHITE KNIGHT** by popular author **Carla Cassidy** (Romance)

On sale January 2000: **THE PREGNANT PRINCESS** by rising star **Anne Marie Winston** (Desire)

On sale February 2000: **MAN…MERCENARY…MONARCH** by top-notch talent **Joan Elliott Pickart** (Special Edition)

ROYALLY WED
Only in—
SILHOUETTE BOOKS

Available at your favorite retail outlet.

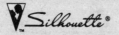

Silhouette ®

Visit us at www.romance.net

SSERW

Start celebrating Silhouette's 20th anniversary with these 4 special titles by *New York Times* bestselling authors

Fire and Rain
by Elizabeth Lowell

King of the Castle
by Heather Graham Pozzessere

State Secrets
by Linda Lael Miller

Paint Me Rainbows
by Fern Michaels

On sale in December 1999

Plus, a special free book offer inside each title!

Available at your favorite retail outlet

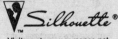

Visit us at www.romance.net

PSNYT